GHOSTS

Ghosts

Putting the Pieces in Place

&

Bloody Baudelaire

by

R. B. Russell

Swan River Press
Dublin, Ireland
MMXXI

Ghosts
by R. B. Russell

Published by
Swan River Press
Dublin, Ireland
in September MMXXI

www.swanriverpress.ie
brian@swanriverpress.ie

Stories © R. B. Russell
Introduction © Mark Valentine
This edition © Swan River Press

Cover design by Meggan Kehrli
from "Lidwine" photograph © yomgaille.com

Set in Garamond by Steve J. Shaw

Paperback Edition
ISBN 978-1-78380-747-5

Swan River Press published
a hardback edition of
Ghosts in February 2012.

Contents

&

Introduction

When I asked a round table of supernatural fiction savants what words came to mind when they thought of R. B. Russell's stories, the answers included "enigmatic", "oblique", "Aickmanesque", "elusive" and "intellectual but accessible" (thanks to John Llewellyn Probert for that one). And it is indeed clear that the work gathered here is a culmination of that rich, resonant strand in the literature of the dark where the reader is taken into uncharted terrain, both physical and psychical.

During the twentieth century, stories of the strange and supernatural began to change. The English ghost story had reached its apogee with the work of M. R. James, who transformed it from its popular, oral, often rather rollicking roots (e.g. in *The Ingoldsby Legends*) to a subtle, scholarly form, laced with irony. However, though James made the mechanisms of the ghost story much finer, he did not interfere with the mainspring of the form. When a spectre, demon, or hellish creature appears, the reader can usually be sure it has an objective existence. The same was true of the stories of the other great writer of supernatural fiction in the early twentieth century, Algernon Blackwood. His stories are often driven by forces of nature, including super-nature, which may be alien and strange to humanity, but are still fully real.

But soon after these stories, there also began to appear work that was not quite so direct. Walter de la Mare, a poet and anthologist of dream-worlds and peculiar visions, was probably the first to write the strange tale in a way which avoided any clear explanation and did not use traditional phenomena in any direct form. Certainly, some of his stories have apparitions, but we are never quite sure about them. It was the borderlands of the mind, as well as those of the spirit, that interested him. The approach that de la Mare used has never been satisfactorily defined: but terms such as the "enigmatic" or "inconclusive" ghost story try to convey the discernible difference between his work and that of M. R. James and his followers.

For many readers, Robert Aickman's strange stories, from later in the century, are in the same prismatic category, wonderfully wrought and capable of being looked at from many angles. He thought the ghost story could, at its best, aspire to the achievements of poetry. The use of delicately placed imagery, of different layers of meaning, the open-endedness of his work, all exemplify what he meant.

The fiction of R. B. Russell seems to me to belong to the same oblique, finely-shaded form that de la Mare and Aickman brought to the strange story. However, his work does not simply follow them, but advances their approach further, mostly because it is written from a more modern sensibility. There are some things his stories often have in common with these predecessors. For example, his protagonists may be emotionally incomplete characters: they are neither satisfied with their own company, nor able to form a strong relationship. Many of de la Mare and Aickman's lead characters are lonely bachelors, rather set in their ways, and possessed of (or by) distinct eccentricities. The well-off scholarly recluse makes his appearance in Russell's stories too, but he gives his similar characters a gentle turn of the screw. His people are not the squires and decayed gentlemen of the forerunners in this form, but often rather gauche, hesitant interlopers in a contemporary world that does not quite work for them.

In the title story of his first collection, "Putting the Pieces in Place", we encounter an obsessive, a literary historian, haunted, figuratively, by a scene and a music he experienced as a young man. His life since has been devoted to the recreation of this. Instead of remaining open to similar, but different, experiences throughout his life, to the possibility of encounters equally as beautiful and compelling, he makes himself (and not entirely metaphorically) the curator of a museum devoted only to this one memory. His mind is over-literal: he collects the things connected with the event, instead of responding to the spirit and essence of what he saw and heard. The story is a subtle meditation on our tendency to enshrine the past instead of engaging with the present. There may not be a definite ghost, in the M. R. James sense, in the story at all: but there certainly is a haunting presence.

The author does not insist on the point, but the thoughtful reader will recognise that the character's rather creepy fixation with an incident and image from his youth is a reproach to the pall of deadening nostalgia that looms over many lives and even, sometimes, entire societies. It is as if the title character of Alain-Fournier's *Le Grand Meaulnes* (a book that Russell admires) had spent his life pursuing, not the lovely young woman he glimpsed at the fête in the lost domain, but all of the props: the costumes, the lanterns, the masks, even the boat on the lake. The effect that the title story achieves is a chilling hollowness, more disturbing than any conventional apparition could ever really be.

In "There's Nothing That I Wouldn't Do", we at first think we are to be introduced to a more confident and unfractured character. The story's framing narrator describes the poise and self-possession of a young architecture student: and not only is she cool-headed and independent, but so are her parents. She moves at ease between international destinations and seems to have a clear career path mapped out. But the reader soon learns to mistrust the narrator who introduces them to this character: for when we encounter Nina, and she takes over telling her story directly, we begin to find that she is apprehensive and ambivalent in her emotional relationships: the outward composure is a screen. As in the architecture she studies, the soaring elevation of her external poise is only one perspective: beneath that there are darker chambers. The story has a macabre, vivid dénouement which cuts into the carefully nuanced narrative of her professional and personal life: a sudden brutal incursion that leaves the reader as disquieted as the narrator. Yet the ultimate terror of the story is perhaps not this gruesome image at its end, but the grey coils of unintention that enmesh us all: the way in which a trail of minor events, each with its own impetus and inevitability, each quite explicable, can nonetheless build to a sudden stark change, a complete re-ordering of an existence. The real horror in the story is the way we may take, all oblivious, a sequence of small steps towards the abyss.

The third piece in this collection, "In Hiding", is an artful story that seems to give us a choice of ghosts, using carefully balanced revelations that leave us never quite certain what we, and the characters, are seeing. But the story is also about other sorts of ghosts: from our past, from the choices we make, from our conscience. It is a fine exemplar of the way in which the modern ghost story form has advanced well beyond the idea of the ghost as simply some sort of post-mortem residue: it is now driven by an understanding that there are far more personal and persistent hauntings within us all. And these new ghosts are much harder to elude. Whatever physical escape we may seek—the equivalent of hiding under the bedsheets or fleeing from the cemetery from the more traditional spirits—this story implies that from our own ghosts there can rarely be any refuge. Like most of R. B. Russell's stories, "In Hiding" is also about shades of grey: the characters have in their past certain deeds not straightforwardly wrong, but neither exactly right: and they remain in a sort of moral limbo, the same ambiguous domain where they now spend their lives.

It is also not only our deeds whose later influence upon us we cannot control: it may equally be the things we imagine. In the poignant and deftly paced story "Eleanor", Russell evokes persuasively what happens to a writer whose one highly successful creation, a *femme fatale*, is taken over by other media: film, television, comics, computer games, so that she is no longer his. In the twilight of his days, tactfully conveyed, this writer strives to find his creation again. We are left with just enough uncertainty about how literally his Eleanor returns to him: but we are also left with a subtle, gentle sense of late decline, of a faltering mind that retains pride in its one great creation. What, we are left to wonder, is the one thing, the one original contribution, that we ourselves will cling to when this decay comes to us too?

The original collection of *Putting the Pieces in Place* concluded with a tale of emotional desolation that was perhaps the bleakest in the book. Jayne in "Dispossessed" has never developed her own life. She has been a barely necessary housekeeper to an elderly lady but does not seem to have ever connected to her employer, the other staff or to her employer's heirs; even her "friends", when they visit her, abuse her trust and take liberties with the house. Her own family is "small and distant". Even when she escapes from this, she soon finds herself in a relationship where she has no real presence: she adapts herself to the tastes and interests of those around her. Her very belongings, such as they are, seem to be meagre and utterly disposable. As in "There's Nothing That I Wouldn't Do", the turns of the story lead to a shocking climax which will linger with the reader: but it is the utter emptiness of Jayne's existence that endures with us even longer

The subtle achievements of the stories in R. B. Russell's first collection are seen also in the striking novella here collected with them: "Bloody Baudelaire". Lucian Miller, the protagonist, confesses that he is in the grip of nostalgia—as we saw in "Putting the Pieces in Place", a single episode involving a beautiful woman and an artistic catalyst has haunted him ever since. The story also introduces us to a memorably obnoxious, and all too realistic, artist, Gerald, haughty and vicious, with a habit of constantly quoting "bloody Baudelaire". Russell portrays him with sharp concision and unerring tone. Like many scoundrels in literature, Gerald is hugely entertaining for the reader: the hapless house guests that are his victims are by contrast too decent, too trained in civilised behaviour, to respond in kind. Lucian is at first embarrassed and uneasy: he is "faltering", "not quite certain", and flinches from the scenes he finds himself in.

Yet as the novella advances, Lucian seems to gain in character while still not deserting his hesitant values, and simply by a sort of awkward persistence, a dogged decency, soon starts to supplant Gerald in everything of consequence—wealth, art, romance, even the future itself. We have the sense that while we are on the surface witnessing a rather messy arty house party, beneath it all a mythic drama is being played out, in which hubris, chance, fate and nemesis have become personified. Great immemorial powers are at large in the house and they are implacable, irrational and unwilling to be appeased until their rite, their ordained drama, has been completed. I think the novella is one of the most original, deeply driven and yet subtly composed contributions to the literature of the strange of the last few decades.

Perhaps, as an early publisher of Ray Russell's fiction, I can hardly claim to be a neutral observer of his work. For the journal *Aklo*, which I edited with Roger Dobson, he provided a fine brief Machenesque tale, "The Pharisee's Glass"; for an anthology of cricketing ghost stories, *Haunted Pavilions*, he obligingly wrote me the evocative and Dunsanyesque "The Holy Game of Cricket", even though he had no particular taste for the game. These and other early stories were the work of a writer affectionate to the classic masters of the field, but still finding his own way. But with "Loup-garou", which Ray contributed to the unpromising vehicle of a werewolf anthology I was editing, we saw strong proof that he was now striking out into his own terrain: and that terrain was strange indeed, mapless, treacherous, changeable, and masked by façades. Ray's justly acclaimed story "Llanfihangel" (published in *Literary Remains*) made use of precisely that metaphor, where the landscapes of borders and liminal places are fused with those of the mind and of the spirit, and where the borders between all these are never very clear.

His characters are already ill at ease with themselves, with others, with the world before any hint of the inexplicable comes on the scene. Often they seem at the mercy of events. Unconfident about their own character, they are also apprehensive about much that is external to them, especially in their relations with other people. Such figures might not draw us to them: but it is the achievement of the author here that in fact we do find them compelling and well worth our attention. I think that is because ultimately, the most persistent quality that R. B. Russell brings to the modern strange tale is a sympathetic identity with human vulnerability.

Mark Valentine

Ghosts

Putting the Pieces in Place

In memory of Grace Russell

The tape came off the first reel, threaded its way through the guides and heads, and flapped uselessly, rhythmically, as the full spool continued to turn. Nicolas Porter opened his eyes at the noise but presumably did not want to believe that the music of Emily Butler had come to an end. Finally, with a smile in the direction of the young woman opposite him and also with a sigh, he got up out of his armchair and walked over to the vintage reel-to-reel machine and switched it off.

"This'll need rewinding, I take it?" he asked.

"As you've only got one tape I wouldn't bother," Beatrice Grant replied. "Just change the two reels over and it's ready to play again."

"But the tape is not now on its original reel!"

"It will be after you've played it next."

He paused and considered:

"I have to admit that I am a little precious about such things. You know what obsessive collectors are like?"

Beatrice Grant said that she didn't, that she had never felt the urge to collect anything, and he gave a short, self-deprecating lecture on how passionate collectors can be about the smallest of things. When he had finished he smiled again, rather guiltily, and said:

"But that did sound absolutely wonderful. It was everything I dreamed it would be. I suppose I should get a copy made; as a back-up?"

"That would be sensible, yes."

"Hmm," he considered, "but no copy will ever sound quite as good as hearing it on that old analogue tape."

"I suppose it's like you reading one of your first editions," she suggested, "on lovely paper, and a nice binding; the words are still the same as in a cheap paperback, but the experience is different."

"I don't know if it is quite the same analogy," he replied, slowly, giving it consideration. "The process of hearing is different. Analogue is warmer, more natural. The bass is thickened up, giving it a fuller sound. It compresses the high end a little too, which is more natural to the ear . . . "

"All right," she held up her hand to stop him. "I believe you. I defer to you in all matters musical as well as literary."

"But you can still tell me what you thought of the music?"

"It was quite beautiful, but classical music isn't my forte, you know? It's obviously very skilful, and sounds romantic . . . The tone is wonderful."

"Emily was playing Mozart's Third, on a reproduction Stradivarius. And we had to listen to this tape on an original RCA reel-to-reel player; I'm pretty sure that's what she would've recorded it on in the first place. I've got a photo of her with this very machine in the background."

"You really are obsessional, aren't you?"

"You don't know the half of it, my dear," he said, with an affected movement of his hand over his brow. "But *you* are the heroine of the hour."

"I couldn't have tracked it down without the information you gave me."

"I have made my living, and my money, by being a literary detective, you know. I have some idea of how these things are done . . . " He turned off the tape player's power at the wall, and then walked over to the bottle of wine which had been warming, open, by the fire. "Now, would you like a glass? We agreed that we wouldn't drink anything until we had heard the tape."

"Yes, please. I think we have something to celebrate, don't you? Although my detective work isn't quite of the same order as yours . . . "

"For me, personally, what you've brought along tonight excels my greatest finds."

"What, even the *Medea*?" she was incredulous.

For Nicolas Porter it was. He knew that the world of classical literature was all the richer for his discovery; he had not needed the eminent figures in the literary world to tell him that. The person that he had been the most pleased to inform of his discovery, though, was his father, who had taught classics at Newcastle University. Porter was secretly pleased to have risen in the old man's estimation; his father had believed his son to be the philistine of the family because he had never been able to hold a pencil, brush or bow. His sisters had been the artistic ones, he was always told, and then he unearthed the full text of Ovid's *Medea* and their achievements had been eclipsed overnight.

"I don't know anything about literature," Beatrice Grant continued, "especially classical literature, but you managed to appear on the front pages of some serious newspapers."

And, he considered, he had earned himself enough money that he no longer needed to haunt provincial auction salerooms, and track down the relicts of authors in the hope of unearthing a cache of unpublished novels.

"I won't ask you how much you got for it . . . ?"

"Good!" he declared, in part because he was not sure that he knew himself; not exactly. He had no idea how much he had spent getting it authenticated, but the debts had kept growing. When he finally sold it at auction the previous year all of the newspapers reported the headline sum, but that was only half of the story. It was bought by an anonymous philanthropist on behalf of a museum, and they'd still not settled the full amount because they had a deal with a publisher who had yet to contribute their payment in lieu of a royalty.

"But will you tell me how you came by it?"

"There are legal reasons why I'd better not."

"Oh." She was slightly crestfallen.

"Well, if I don't name names . . . " he agreed. "It is incredibly convoluted because the collector who owned it had originally acquired it from an institution thirty years ago. As far as *they* knew it was just some early Latin manuscript, and the collector who bought it from them didn't know any better for the first few years. When he came to read it he had his suspicions that it was copied from a far earlier Greek source, but I don't think he ever got it authenticated. When I discovered, from the records of that institution, exactly who they had sold it to, I asked the owner if I could see it, but he refused. He wasn't one of those collectors who like to share their treasures, even to impress, or to make other collectors envious. Then, when he died, his widow sold it to me, knowing that it had value, but not knowing what on earth it was."

"And the problem is?"

"Not only is the widow who sold me the *Medea* threatening to take me to court, claiming I should have paid her more, but the original institution who sold it to her husband is threatening to do the same."

"Will they get anywhere?"

"I don't know, and frankly, at this very moment I don't care."

"But you're still happy that you've paid me ten thousand pounds for the tape now that you've listened to it?"

"Of course! I haven't heard that music for forty years and it still sounds wonderful."

"You mean, you've heard it before?"

"Yes, I've heard it before. There was a very sentimental reason for wanting that tape. And I've reached an age, and financial comfort, that allows me to indulge such sentimentality. Let me show you."

He put down his wine and walked over to a case on a table next to a music stand. With great care and reverence he took out a violin.

"This is the very instrument that Emily Butler plays on that recording."

"How on earth did you track that down?" she asked, standing up to take a look, although he possessively kept hold of it.

"I have a contact in the world of violins who is the counterpart of me in the literary world. You see, although it isn't a Stradivarius, as was thought for many years, it is a very good, early copy, and has a lovely sound. Really good violins need provenance, and this one came up with an impeccable record of ownership. I know for a fact that it was hers."

"You really are an obsessive . . . "

"You don't know the half of it!"

"Surprise me."

"All right. How about if I told you that this house was once where she lived?"

Beatrice Grant laughed at this: "I am seriously impressed. I suppose there was a certain amount of luck involved, though."

"In what way?"

"In the house becoming available?"

"For all collectors there's some luck, but if you are serious you usually have to persuade people to make things become available, and not just wait. But in the case of this house, it had been empty for years."

"What, a desirable property like this?"

"Yes, but it has some serious drawbacks."

"In what way?"

"The whole of the front façade has subsided and should really be rebuilt. It would be cheaper to pull the whole place down and start again, but it's Listed and the planners wouldn't hear of it. And so it's been allowed to decay, and has inevitably fallen into a worse and worse condition. And, of course, it has the reputation of being haunted."

"Splendid! What kind of ghost? . . . Not your violin player?"

He looked slightly uncomfortable.

"It is!" she clapped her hands with delight. "You are the most committed collector I've ever come across. It's not good enough just to have her music, and the instrument she played it on, or even the house she lived in, but you must have her ghost as well!"

"So," she asked, after a suitable pause, "have you seen her?"

He looked up at the ceiling and admitted, reluctantly, that he had not.

"But it's not a visual ghost," he explained. "It's an audible one. It is said that music can sometimes be heard coming from this house."

"Violin music?"

"Of that I'm not sure. You see, I've asked around and although everyone knows the story, I can't find anyone who will admit to having heard anything themselves."

"Are the stories recent?"

"I never heard them when I was living in the area, up to the early seventies. Emily drowned in a tragic boating accident in 1975, and I assume the stories date from after that . . ."

"So, how long have you been living here?"

"Only a couple of months. I bought the place a year ago, but it's taken that long for the builders to make it habitable again."

She sat back down in her chair and savoured the delicious tale.

"You do realise that your ghost isn't likely to play any music for you? Not if you are constantly listening out for her?"

"I know, I know. And the odds are that if I not only heard but saw the ghost, I'd discover that it was her mother, or her father. The thing is, I don't even believe in ghosts. I've never seen one, and don't really expect to."

"But, you'd be happy to meet a ghost if she happened to be the right one?"

"Of course."

He put the violin carefully back into its case and turned his attention to the bottle of wine. When he had refilled their glasses he sat back down again in his chair and she prompted him:

"So, you heard her play the violin in the . . . " she made the calculation, " . . . late sixties?"

"Yes. I suppose I was one of the very first to hear her. It was at a party, like in *Le Grand Meaulnes*. You know the book? I was about fourteen and had been out on a long walk on a hot August day. I'd gone miles, and was coming back down the Dale when I heard this wonderful, unearthly music. It wasn't like anything I'd ever experienced before. It was odd, but I couldn't immediately identify it as being from a violin. I was a romantic lad . . . And I heard this yearning, longing music floating through the descending twilight of a warm summer's evening . . . "

Porter had replayed the memory so often in his mind that he feared it was a highly romanticised and unrealistic account that he remembered, although he was sure the salient facts were correct. When he had first heard the music he hadn't immediately understood where it was coming from, but further down the Dale he could see coloured lights. As he got closer he realised that there was a party, and when the music stopped and there was applause, he knew that he had come to the right place. He had to cross a few fields where he was unsure who the owner was, but then he was on the edge of their garden looking at all these people in summer clothes, all appearing somehow very refined and magical. They were not local.

He didn't know how long he watched them, but eventually a young woman appeared in a white flowing dress, and she played the violin again. It was beautiful, thrilling, moving . . .

"I was sure that nobody else at the party was appreciating her music like I was. I thought she was the most wonderful woman I'd ever seen in my life, and her music the most beautiful I'd heard. She would have been seventeen at the time . . . "

He eventually tore himself away. He had waited for hours in the hope that she might play once more, but she had not.

"I asked around and found out who she was," Porter explained to his visitor. "And a few weeks later I turned up on the doorstep of her house, this house, with some excuse for making myself known to the family. Only, I was told that she had just left for London, where she had a place with an orchestra."

"Did you ever meet her?"

"No. I tried to follow her career, but she didn't get to play any of the major first violin or solo material until just before she died. She was never properly recorded; apparently she was just about to go into the studio when the accident happened."

"So, are there many other collectors out there?"

"No, because they haven't known that there was anything to collect. But I haven't yet asked you how easily you came by the recording?"

Beatrice Grant had been patiently waiting for the opportunity to tell him of her part in the story.

"Well, you told me that her brother had disposed of the contents of the family home at an auction, and that's where the tape might have gone." She took her time, proud of her detective work: "The auction records hadn't survived, but I was told about a man who ran a large junk shop in Penrith. At that time he used to make offers for the unsold lots after auction and a good proportion of the items nobody else wanted passed through his hands. The odds on the tape recording going to him were very poor, but there was always the possibility of it. Well, he remembered the tape very clearly. You see, he kept a reel-to-reel player from an unsold lot and there had been a tape of violin music on it. There weren't any other tapes with it, and he hadn't any of his own, so he used to play the same one over and over again in his shop. He said that he loved the music, but one day a customer came in and liked it so much that he bought it. Luckily the owner knew who the man was; someone called Bathgate. And though this Bathgate had moved to Venice I managed to track him down."

"What wonderful detective work," Nicolas bowed his head. "I hope that you didn't have to pay this man too much for the tape?"

"I assume that like the lady who sold you the *Medea*, Bathgate didn't know quite what it was he had. You told me to tell him that I was a member of Emily Butler's family, but to try not to go into details."

"I did."

"Well, he acted very oddly when he saw me. He wanted to know why I was there, and I told him what I wanted. He rushed off and couldn't come back with it quickly enough. Strangely, though, after such a strange display, he seemed to want me to stay, but he was getting a bit creepy by then. Once I had the tape I left as quickly as I could."

"The poor fellow," Porter replied, shaking his head.

"How much I may or may not have paid for it is my own affair," she said defensively.

"Don't worry, the money really is immaterial," he assured her. "To me that tape is worth so much more than anything else I have; more than her violin, or even this house." He paused and looked around him: "You know, I call this the music room. This was where they'd have recorded the tape. There's a photo, a family group, taken in this room. I've recreated the details as faithfully as I can."

"If the ghost feels at home she might deign to make an appearance?"

"You never know. Every night I wind up the clock and lock the doors. I have a little routine. And I pass this room on my way to the foot of the stairs and I invariably get a frisson as I pass the door. If I don't actually look in I feel that someone may be in here."

"And if you *do* look properly?"

He laughed loudly: "Then there's nothing at all. It took me some days to realise that the impression is caused by that mirror over there. My eyesight is not as it should be, and the figure I see out of the corner of my eye is my own reflection. You know, if I get up in the night I always pop down the stairs and listen, but I've never heard a sound."

"I'm not sure whether to admire your dedication, or despair at it," she told him, and he laughed again, and then decided that it must be time to eat.

&

Nicolas Porter was not so much a collector who was obsessive; rather he was an obsessive who happened to be a collector. Neurotic about his appearance, the tidiness of his house (and even his accounts, he assured her), he was equally fastidious about his food. He had been busy cooking all afternoon he claimed, and ever since she had arrived he had continually checked his watch and disappeared off to the kitchen where he told her he was preparing his speciality dish. The smells that came through to where she waited were quite irresistible.

He suggested she browse in his library for a quarter of an hour, before he came back and sat her down in the dining room and was almost immediately gone again. When he returned he brought with him what he called salt crust baked duck. The meat was tasty, although nearly overwhelmed by the vanilla orange sauce which he had served with it. Porter admitted that the sauce was slightly too strong, but Beatrice Grant was just as surprised by the fennel and citrus salad with which he seemed to be pleased. He had asked her to try the "off-dry Vouvray" before pouring her a full glass, and though she knew little about such matters it did seem the perfect accompaniment.

Later, when he brought out the chocolate brioche dessert, they changed wines again, but this time he did not offer her a taster.

"I always drink Chateau d'Yquem with dessert," he insisted. "Or, at least, I have done since I sold the *Medea*!"

They finished with a large glass of Calvados which they drank at the table, neither of them being inclined to move back into the living room.

"I haven't been entirely honest with you, though," Porter admitted. They had talked on any number of different subjects while they had eaten, but it was obvious that he had returned to the matter of the tape that she had acquired for him. "I must apologise, but some of the lines of enquiry that you undertook I also followed up, a couple of years ago."

"Why didn't you tell me?"

"I knew you'd approach Bathgate in the right frame of mind if you'd had to work for it first. And also if you did not know everything that I did."

"You knew that Bathgate had the tape?"

He nodded.

"So I didn't really need to tramp around auction houses and travel to Penrith? Looking up Bathgate wasn't hard, but presumably you could have arranged for an introduction to the man for me?"

"No, not quite. You see, I asked the same questions as you at the auction house, went to Penrith and on to Bathgate. I found him in Venice but he wasn't happy to see me."

"None of this makes sense."

"It will, it will."

He looked into his glass for perhaps a minute and then told her the story.

§

Statistically speaking, he explained, coincidences have to occur; if they didn't then something must be conspiring to order the world unnaturally. And if one looks into the statistics of this case it wasn't really that unlikely that Oliver Bathgate would happen to walk into a large cluttered junk shop and hear the tape of Emily Butler playing her violin. Porter told her that she had to allow for the fact that the owner of the shop played it regularly; he appreciated the quality of the only piece of music he had in the shop. And Oliver Bathgate was an antiques dealer, and in his time would have visited antiques shops all over Britain. However, even if one accepts that it was not unlikely that he would hear the music, it would have been the last thing that he would have himself expected to discover by chance.

Bathgate had bought it from the owner, and when Porter visited the shop a few years later the man remembered Bathgate very well. His memory was especially clear because his customer had paid him a hundred pounds for the tape. And he had left a forwarding address, in case anything else turned up. He was so concerned that something else might surface from the sale of the Butler family's estate that when he later moved to Venice he wrote to the owner of the shop with his new address.

So there were no outrageous coincidences, Porter told his guest, and the trail was laid pretty easily for him to follow, as it was for her afterwards. And as she had so recently done, he found his way to Venice to track down Bathgate, and like her Porter knew nothing about the man . . . That is, until he got there.

"Did you know Venice before you visited?" Porter asked her. "It is a wonderful city."

"I was only there for a couple of hours," she admitted. "As soon as I had the tape in my hands I was off to the mainland to catch a flight home!"

"I'm glad you came straight here."

"I wanted to be paid the balance of my fee!"

"When *I* went to see Bathgate I was on the same mission as you, but I did not find him at home when I first arrived . . . " Porter looked back happily on his two weeks in Venice. He had rented an apartment and while he had waited he visited the palaces associated with Byron and Corvo, Proust and Casanova. On the very first day he went to the Ponta Bergami and stared at the sad façade of the Palazzo Capello; the setting for Henry James's *The Aspern Papers*. The building was in a poor state of repair, as though untenanted since the time of Miss Bordereau and her niece. Porter often considered that his whole career was based on the slender plot of that story.

"How long did you expect to wait for Bathgate?" she asked him.

"However long it took!" Porter was there with the intention of playing his "long game". It was a tactic he had used to his advantage in many of his discoveries; a tactic that did have something underhanded about it, he admitted to himself. All of his literary finds had been the result of almost infinite patience. Unearthing the *Medea* itself had been the result of ten years of work.

Porter had arrived at Bathgate's address every morning by a narrow *calle* alongside a high-walled garden belonging to a neighbour.

"Well," he continued, "after a week Bathgate himself was finally at home to respond to my knocking. He answered through the intercom and I said that I was from England. He was happy to let me in."

Porter had, in fact, lied. He told Bathgate that he had known him many years before, and the lock of the door had shot open with a hollow sound from inside. And so Porter found himself in that same dark, cavernous and cold hall that Beatrice Grant had recently experienced. He was confronted by the same intimidating marble staircase that climbed up at a right angle, and when he ventured in he saw Bathgate standing at the head of the stairs, silhouetted against an unshuttered window.

"Welcome to my Palace," Bathgate had said, dramatically. "Although it is only a small one, and some experts insist on calling it a *Palazzo* . . . " He had not seemed quite so tall when Porter had reached him on the landing above.

"He's a dapper man with grey hair and a goatee beard?" Beatrice Grant checked.

"That was him. Did you go up to his apartments?"

"We conducted all of our business down in the hall," she said.

"Then, you missed out on a treat."

Porter had been envious. Bathgate's *palazzo* was wonderful; he took his visitor into the main room which was decorated with eclectic and fantastic artwork, and wooden and plaster angels, presumably looted from churches. And the view from his windows! The bright sun shone on the Grand Canal, and each building flanking it was an architectural wonder; even the most mundane of craft on the jaunty waters were transformed into things of splendour. Further up the waterway the crowds of tourists on the Academia Bridge seemed no longer gauche and annoying, but looked like celebrants in some mystery play.

"My Palace has a picturesque history of ill-fortune," Bathgate told Porter, "although the majority of its previous owners have all died comfortably in their beds at a very old age. I love its splendidly unbalanced façade. Unfortunately the coloured marble was cleaned and restored by its last owner . . . "

Porter admitted that his host had then apologised for not knowing exactly who his guest was, or why he was there.

"I told him the truth," Porter insisted to Grant. "I said that I had been born and brought up in the same Dale as Emily Butler. I told him that I had heard her play her violin when I was a teenager, and that I had been bewitched by it."

Porter had also told Bathgate that the two of them had met at that summer party, when she had played. He did not mention that he had spied on the gathering from the outside. He claimed that he had talked to Bathgate, but it was so long ago that it was natural the man had forgotten. Porter told him that he had found out, quite by chance, that Bathgate had a recording of Emily playing the violin. The visitor to Venice claimed that he simply happened to be there on holiday and had decided to look him up.

There were problems with the explanation, of course, and Porter was prepared to continue lying to shore up his shaky story, but Bathgate was not interested in discussing them. He walked back to the window, to his view, and stood contemplating it for several minutes.

Bathgate said: "I was paralysed when I first heard that tape. I was transported back fifteen years in time to that bright party where Emily had so impressed everyone by her playing. As I stood there in that rubbishy antique shop I was convinced that I was going mad; having an hallucination."

Bathgate admitted, quite candidly, that around the time of that party he had taken LSD, and twice he had later experienced frightening flashbacks, even though it was years since he had stopped experimenting with the drug. He said that those experiences were something like that; his heart raced, his mouth was dry and he nearly fell over. The man who owned the junk shop sat him down and brought him a glass of water. Eventually Bathgate asked about the music and the owner explained how he had acquired it. The customer was still trembling when he left the shop carrying the tape.

"And when you played it?" Porter had asked Bathgate.

"I never have . . . I was in my house in London at the time. I bought a tape player and sat there on my own, with it all set up before me. I made certain that nobody would interrupt me, but I couldn't bring myself to turn it on. I sat up late into the night, always about to play it, but never quite having the courage to do so. It was after that night that I resolved to move back to Venice."

"But why couldn't you play it?" Porter asked.

Bathgate had not answered him, but looked out over the canal once more. Finally he started to talk, and at first Porter assumed that he was changing the subject:

"Venice is the most beautiful city in the world," he said. "People come here to forget, but it isn't a city that allows forgetfulness. It is inconceivably old and every day that passes is recorded in its stones, in its bricks and crumbling plaster. But, despite its apparent, eternal decomposition, it remains standing . . . And those old warm bricks that shrug off the damp plaster to gaze narcissistically into these stinking jade green canals have always looked backwards . . . And so the inhabitants of Venice must also dwell in the past . . . "

"I should not stay here," he continued, "because the past can never be forgotten here. But in this city a personal tragedy may take comfort amidst the clamour of so many other painful histories. The insistence of my own story cannot be drowned out by those others, but it might find a kind of companionship."

And then Bathgate had laughed, slightly hysterically: " 'Drowned out'; that's an unfortunate choice of words," he said. "Unfortunate when Emily died by drowning."

Then he turned and asked if Porter knew who he was.

"Oliver Bathgate?" he had lamely replied.

"But do you know why I have the tape, and what it means to me? Do you know what Emily Butler meant to me, and what I meant to her?"

Porter admitted that he didn't.

"Do you have any idea of the circumstances surrounding her death?"

He mumbled that he knew nothing aside from the fact that there had been a boating accident.

"Yes, an accident. And it happened here, in Venice."

Bathgate had walked over to Porter, threateningly, and stood with his face uncomfortably close to his. Porter had to back away.

"She went over the side of my launch, while I was piloting it." A pause, then, "You didn't know that, did you?"

"I'm sorry. No, I didn't."

"And don't you think that it makes me feel just a little bit guilty?" he asked, with sarcasm in his voice.

"Of course."

"Of course!" he shouted, and the words echoed around the lofty room. "There hasn't been a day that's gone by without me knowing that I am the most miserable wretch on earth. I'd been drinking, you see. We were out on the lagoon and when she went over the side I didn't realise. I just kept going, way past the speed limit. And when I did notice, when I knew for certain what a horrible, horrible thing had happened, could I find her? I was too disorientated and befuddled to know where I'd been going. It was all I could do to get to the bright lights of St. Mark's and call for help . . . And you want me to give you the only thing of Emily's that I have?"

"I understand," Porter had quietly said.

"Of course you don't understand!" Bathgate almost screamed.

❧

Porter looked at Beatrice Grant, sitting opposite him:

"They had been in love, and he killed her. And now that he had the tape he couldn't bring himself to listen to it. He said that every note that she played on it would reproach him for what he had done to her."

"The poor man."

"Yes, but then he said that he sometimes thought that it would be better for everybody if he just threw it away! I cried out 'Don't do that, for God's sake!' and he asked why not? He asked who the hell I was? He said that I wasn't even family. If I was, apparently, he'd have been happy to hand the tape over to me . . . And at that moment I knew that a dignified exit was required."

Porter's guest thought that she could see what had happened: "That's why you told me to say that I was a member of the family when I asked for the tape?" she said.

"Exactly."

"But why didn't Bathgate at least ask who I was? Or how I was related? Why didn't he ask for proof?"

"Was he scared when he saw you?"

"Scared? Well, shaken, yes. He behaved very oddly."

"There is a little more to explain," Porter said. "I knew that I would have to send somebody else to get the tape for me, and I had to make certain that the odds on that person succeeding were maximised."

"And you allowed for something else? You expected him to be scared of me?"

"I threw something else into the equation that I hoped would help the story that you were a relative of Emily's."

"You asked me to do this because I look like her, don't I?"

He grinned broadly:

"I asked you to track down the tape for me because I knew you were clever, and you've just proved it, again. That was important; without your intelligence it would have mattered little that there was a family resemblance."

"Can I see a photograph of her?"

"Of course. I normally have a few around the house but I tidied them away when you phoned to say that you were coming. I didn't want to worry you."

"Worry me? Now I understand. I look a lot like her, don't I? That was why Bathgate was so rattled when he saw me."

"There is a striking resemblance."

"Perhaps I should be worried? You have her music, her violin, her house, perhaps even her ghost. And then I come along, looking just like her, and I am in your debt by ten thousand pounds . . . "

"I promise that it is me, not you, who is in debt here. Without you I would have no tape. You must remember that I am an *obsessive* collector. Second best wouldn't be good enough . . . "

"And I would be second best?"

"You are delightful; pretty, intelligent, interesting . . . But you are not Emily Butler."

He got up and walked to a bureau from which he brought out a framed photograph which he passed to Beatrice. Emily Butler had looked a lot like her, she could see that.

"In the half-light of Bathgate's entrance hall you would have appeared to be her double," Porter explained.

"Or her ghost?"

"I didn't know what he would do, but I knew that he would be shocked to see you. When I was looking for somebody to go out there for me I was only hoping for what might pass for a family resemblance. It took me two years to find you, and I almost didn't ask because you looked too much like Emily."

Porter gave Beatrice Grant the master bedroom for herself that night. She did wonder who was in Emily's old room, but she didn't ask; it wouldn't have been beyond him to discover which one it had been. She did not quite know what to think of the man, and with his generous payment for the tape she didn't feel that she had much right to criticise him in any way. She was annoyed that he had not told her more before she went out to see Bathgate, but perhaps she would have behaved differently if she had known more about Emily Butler's resemblance to her. Grant was sure that she would have behaved differently in front of Bathgate if she had known then what she now knew about his history. Grant consoled herself with the fact that no matter how much more of a right Bathgate had to that tape, it was not as though he had ever listened to it and appreciated it. And did he really deserve any sympathy when he was probably responsible for her death? Porter's morality was suspect, but she did not feel concerned about being alone in the same house as him; she believed him when he said he was not interested in her. His obsession was with Emily Butler, and perhaps it was no more strange than the obsessions of many collectors. Porter simply had the money to indulge his passion to an extreme that others could not consider.

When she went to wash in the bathroom she could hear him downstairs in the kitchen, clearing up after his wonderful meal, and she wondered whether she should have offered to help. However, she was so tired after her recent flights to and from Venice, and from the long drive up to Yorkshire, that all she wanted to do was sleep. When she was safely back in her room she undressed and got in between the cold sheets. She was wondering about the psychology of paying her so much money for what could have been a simple errand, when she must have fallen asleep. She couldn't judge the time at all but it was dark when she woke again, and she felt uncomfortable from all of the rich food she had eaten. She could hear the music again from downstairs but was not surprised that Porter was presumably unable to stop listening to it. Her first thought was that it was rather too loud and if she wanted to get back to sleep then she would have to go down and ask him to lower the volume.

Her mind was racing a little. She was too warm now and unable relax not only because of all the food, and the wine that she had drunk. She was beginning to be annoyed by her host, but a little later the music did stop. She waited to hear him come up the stairs. Had he fallen asleep down there? She didn't know the time; she hadn't a watch and there was no clock that she could see. She seemed to be lying there for hours, unable to sleep, despite her tiredness. She became even more irritated when she realised that she needed to have a pee, and she got up, hoping that she would not encounter her host on the landing.

The house was now completely quiet, and when she came out from the bathroom she stood there and let her eyes get used to the dark, deciding that it was a friendly, family house, and wishing that she might have somehow known Emily Butler herself. She wondered whether Porter was one of those collectors who would really share his treasures? She hoped that he might make her a copy of the music that he had been so thrilled to finally own?

Beatrice Grant remembered what Porter had said about going downstairs and taking a look in the music room. She decided that she would do the same, and she would get herself a glass of milk from his kitchen while she was down there. She reasoned that she had to forget about her need for sleep if she was ever to allow herself to succumb to it.

The moon was shining brightly through the landing window and picked out the stairs for her. The hall below was darker, but light was obviously coming in through the windows of the rooms at the front of the house. She was thinking about the glass of milk as she walked past the music room and at the edge of her vision she saw something move. She looked back in and saw her reflection in the mirror and smiled at the illusion. Poor Nicolas Porter would never see Emily as those features stared back at Beatrice, even in the dimmest light.

She peered at the smiling reflection in the gloom, and saw that she appeared to be wearing something black, with a collar, buttoned high at the neck. She looked down at herself in surprise and confirmed that she was still wearing her white nightdress. In an instant she looked back up at the reflection where the woman in the mirror was now wearing the nightdress.

Beatrice Grant's legs suddenly felt weak. She was not scared by what she thought she had seen, but she had no idea of what to make of it. She clutched the door frame and could not take her eyes off the mirror which was certainly now showing a true reflection. She was terrified a second later, however, when a quiet voice from within the dark room said, simply:

"Thank you."

She backed away from the door, trembling from head to foot. A chair creaked from inside the room, as somebody unmistakably stood up. And then walking towards her from the shadows was a dark figure. She pressed herself against the wall she had backed into, and when the silhouetted form reached the door it switched on a light and was revealed to be Porter.

Her heart crashed in her chest, but she was able to breathe again, not having done so for several seconds.

"Thank you," he repeated, smiling.

"What did you see?" she asked, trying to control her voice.

"A reflection in the mirror," he replied simply.

"Whose?"

He shrugged. "What I thought I saw for a moment, and what I actually did see, might not be the same thing. Who knows? What did you see?"

"I don't know. I don't know at all."

"That's all right," he said calmly, reassuring her that he would not ask again.

"Were you waiting for me to come down?" she questioned him.

"I hoped that you might come down earlier, when I was playing the music. When you didn't, I waited."

"Did you know what would happen if I did?"

"No, not at all. But the way that I work, as a collector, is to put the various elements of a situation together in such a way as may be advantageous. Then I observe the results. As I said earlier this evening, for all collectors there has to be an element of luck, but if you are serious you usually have to choreograph or arrange a situation, and persuade people to make things happen. It is not good enough just to wait, and hope."

And with that he said goodnight, switched off the light, and walked towards the stairs, to finally retire for the evening.

There's Nothing I Wouldn't Do

Most people seem to consider Nina Monkman to be a self-assured, confident young woman, but I have known her long enough to realise that this is not quite the truth. Her appearance of self-belief has often got her a long way, and it is something I have always admired and rather envied about her. I did meet her parents a few years ago and it was obvious that this is a family trait; they are also calm, confident people, and they have passed this on to their only daughter. None of them are arrogant; they are open and friendly, and I have always been a little jealous of their poise.

I first met Nina at school and we happened, by chance, to go up to the same University, where she studied architecture. After three years there it was just like her to decide to take her first year working in practice in Sweden, rather than remain in the city. She returned for two years to complete her M.A., but then spent her next year back in practice in Brazil. It would never have occurred to her that moving to a foreign country, where she did not know the language, would cause any difficulties, and she seems to have enjoyed both experiences.

Nina returned to England and spent a further year in the offices of a large architecture practice in London before taking her exams and qualifying, but I know that she found this last part of her education rather dull. I was therefore very surprised when she announced that she was going to study for a PhD. The only people I knew who had taken this course had been attached to the University where they had trained, but, inevitably, that was not Nina's intention. She had come across a Ukrainian architect whose recent work interested her and she had decided to go to a University in his country. Although the Berlin Wall had come down a few years previously the idea of anybody going to live in Eastern Europe, albeit temporarily, was surprising. It was only a few weeks after making her decision that she left England again, now bound for Odessa.

We received letters and cards from Nina, but on her return at Christmas she expressed reservations about returning to the Ukraine the following term. It was unlike her to be so negative, and on our first reunion she refused to explain why she was so unwilling to go back. She was not her usual, buoyant self, but we felt it prudent not to ask too many questions at that point. Early in January, though, she stayed with me for a couple of days and was still evidently on edge and worried about something. With reluctance she agreed to explain.

That evening, as she sat in the armchair opposite me with a large glass of wine, she said that the problem was a young man called Taras.

"I'm sure I met him on the first day that I arrived in Odessa," she said, "He was not good-looking and I didn't really 'notice' him until one day at the end of October when a whole group of us went on a picnic. It was unseasonably hot and we knew there may not be another fine day available to us that year. A merry procession of students took the train out to some dreary suburb and we walked up an interminable hill. I followed behind them with a heavy heart."

"You weren't happy there, even then?"

Nina shook her head, took a deep breath, and told me what had happened:

℘

No, I was not happy, but when we got to the top of that hill we were suddenly in the countryside. They all ran, shouting, down this tree-lined road and for a moment I forgot my troubles and ran with them.

At the bottom of the valley a wide, shallow, clear river pushed through the fields and this was what we were all evidently making for. At the bridge everybody climbed the fence and ran down to the pebbly bank where, with few exceptions, the students stripped down to their underclothes. With squeals and shouts they ran to the water and threw themselves in. I kicked off my shoes, tucked my dress in my pants, and rushed in after them. But the water was so cold that it hurt my legs. They ached so profoundly that I very nearly stumbled and fell, so I turned around and made my way out as quickly as I could. I walked awkwardly over the pebbles and up to a patch of grass in the sun. I sat down next to Taras, an English student.

"This is a lovely place?" he suggested, his accent sounding slightly American.

I agreed that it was, pleased to hear my own language spoken for the first time that day. I chaffed my legs to try and warm them.

"Every weekend," he said, carefully selecting his words, "We say, 'let us go to the river'. All summer we have said it, and never came. But finally we are here."

"It's beautiful."

"And the city is so ugly."

I could not quite agree with him. The city is, in fact, very beautiful: at least in the centre. Fine eighteenth and nineteenth century buildings have survived the Soviet replanning, and many streets are delightfully lined with trees. A cosmopolitan port, it has never been of any military significance and so the old harbour has never been redeveloped. It retains a charm that surprised me when I first arrived two months before. The university buildings are likewise beautiful, and from inside them the views out down the wide streets and boulevards are elegant and impressive. My Hall of Residence is something entirely different, though; a mile from the city centre, it is a dark, oppressive essay in decaying concrete. It doesn't help that the Hall is so noisy; as a post-graduate of twenty-four I find that the eighteen-year-olds in the Hall already seem a whole generation younger than me.

One of my main grievances is that fewer people speak English there than I'd been led to believe. I was told that at the University, of all places, it would be the international language, but this isn't so in the architecture department. I do, finally, have a supervising tutor who speaks English. But English doesn't appear to be spoken at all outside of the University. I suppose I was fortunate to have a room in a corridor in the Hall of Residence with several English Language students, of whom Taras was one.

On that day we first talked:

"We will swim here," he said, "but we must not start eating and drinking until lunchtime."

"Why's that?"

"If we start now we will finish the food and beer too soon. And then some will return, and the party is finished . . . " He smiled and lay back on the grass, closing his eyes. "Tell me again; who is the architect you are studying?"

"Alexander de Saussure," I told him.

"I said that to my tutor, but he has never heard of him either."

"He's very fashionable in England," I told him, with a little obvious bitterness.

"Then the answer is that we are not fashionable here in Ukraine?"

"I have a horrible feeling, that when I go back to England, he will no longer be in fashion there either."

"Then," he said, choosing his words, still with his eyes closed, and smiling as he found the right phrase, "You will be a fashion victim!"

He laughed, and it hurt that he was right. It had been my fear from the moment that I descended the steps from the aeroplane and looked at the horrible nineteen-sixties airport building. I'd been seduced by some carefully selected photographs in a couple of architectural magazines, and had fallen for some excitable articles which suggested that de Saussure was soon going to be an architect with a great international reputation. He'd won a competition for an arts centre in The Hague and the drawings that had been published, alongside the explanation of his design philosophy, had convinced me that my career could be made by clutching on to this man's coat-tails. A year in the Ukraine studying his work and a few interviews with the great man himself appeared to me to be an easy way to obtain some more initials after my name, and hopefully a position in a good architecture practice. However, I admit that my enthusiasm may have clouded my judgment. It was only when I had arrived that I realised that his own practice had churned out a whole series of uninspired commercial buildings prior to his high-profile competition win. The philosophical underpinning to his work did not appear to relate to anything he had previously designed.

"Me and my friends," Taras mused, "are studying English so that we can leave Ukraine and get good jobs in interesting countries. But you, you come to Odessa when you could remain in England! You are very strange."

"It seemed like a good idea at the time," I sighed, and as I did so he opened his eyes and his brow wrinkled into a frown.

"You are not happy here?" he asked.

"No, not completely."

Taras sat up and took my hand, staring gravely into my face.

"What can we do to make you happy?"

"I don't know. Perhaps I should just pack my bags and go home?"

And then he kissed me. It was a nice kiss, a sensuous kiss. I did not think Taras good-looking, I was not attracted to him, but at that moment the contact and the warmth were so welcome that I responded. I closed my eyes, which I almost never do when I kiss.

Somebody wolf-whistled from the direction of the river and Taras pulled away, looking over to where most of the other students were still horsing around in the water. I lay down and a moment later he laid beside me, taking my hand in his.

"I would like to help you," he said with a sincerity that made me feel uncomfortable, for I was rather equivocal about our sudden intimacy.

"I'm just in a bad mood," I said.

"Okay," he replied, but I was unable to interpret his meaning. He said nothing more and as we lay there I became concerned that I had offended him.

I moved onto my side and propped myself up on my elbow, supporting my head on my hand, and looking down at him. He was staring up at the underside of the trees. He was pale, dark-haired and rather skinny. I was worried about the difference in our ages; he seemed so young.

A bird flew over us and for a second he watched it. I looked into his eyes and they seemed very sad. I realised that telling him how miserable I was just after we had kissed had been tactless. To make amends I said:

"There are some good things about being here."

"Like what?" he asked, expressionless.

"You," I lied, or half-lied, for I suppose that I did like him. I was grateful for his company.

He considered for a few moments and then looked into my face, scrutinising me and, I assumed, doubting me. This annoyed me, so I added.

"I do like you very much."

I wasn't going to go any further, and I certainly wasn't going to say that I found him attractive because that would have been very wrong. But my awkward words might have implied this, and he smiled and sat up.

"I like you as well," he announced. "And I want to make you happy. And you make me happy."

I was pleased at his reaction. He looked about him and smiled broadly:

"It is a beautiful day, and a beautiful place. And I am in love with a beautiful woman from England."

There was something about the way he announced this that pleased me. I was flattered, I suppose. All in all, the sounds of laughter and shouting from the river, and the sun's warmth as we sat on the grass, all meant that continuing to kiss Taras was an easy and a pleasant way to spend the rest of the afternoon.

I had no intention to deceive him, but that is exactly what I did. I acted out of motives that I am not at all proud of. I enjoyed that afternoon in the countryside, with the food and drink and the light-hearted company. I enjoyed the fact that Taras had said he loved me and thought me beautiful. Yes, he was a skinny young thing and had features that I can only describe as bland, but I did not put much thought into what happened. I knew that in any other situation I would have declined his attentions, but I did not feel that I had a choice if I wanted to feel close to someone in that foreign country; and that was exactly what I wanted at that moment.

But following that afternoon I took to avoiding Taras. I was a little embarrassed, and I felt rather guilty. And then, one night a week later, he knocked at the door of my room while I was sitting inside at my desk working. I recognised his voice as he had said goodbye to a friend a few doors away and I had listened to his steps in the corridor as he had approached the door to my room.

I sat still, saying nothing, and he knocked again and quietly called my name. I knew he could not open the door from the outside and simply come in, and although my light was on he could not be sure that I was inside. I decided to pretend to be out.

"I know you're there," he said hopefully, and I was worried that perhaps he had been outside and had seen my silhouette against the curtain.

"If you do not want to see me any more, I understand," he said, slightly pathetically.

I did not like being so cruel, but decided that I should continue with the pretence; he couldn't know for certain that I was inside and it would hurt him less if I carried on the charade rather than answer the door and confirm his suspicions.

And then I heard no more. If he was still standing outside, listening, I could not tell, but I had not heard him walk away. Noiselessly I moved into a more comfortable position and continued to read the book from which I'd been taking notes. Five minutes passed, ten, and then I heard the door banging at the end of the corridor and footsteps came down and past my door, not stopping until they reached a position much further down the corridor where another door opened and closed. As they had passed by my room no words had been exchanged with Taras, if he was still there, and their pace had not changed as they walked by.

It seemed likely that he had gone, but I nevertheless got out of my chair very quietly and lay down on the bed to try and read a magazine. It must have been nearly a quarter of an hour later that I heard a group of two or three people walking down the corridor, and again they made no allowance for anybody standing outside of my door. I was feeling terribly guilty by this time and I decided that I would have to make it up to Taras. I resolved to go to his room, pretending that I had been elsewhere and had just that moment returned. I would invite him to the Hall bar for a drink.

I immediately felt much better for the idea, got up and put on my shoes. I let myself quietly out of my door, and there he was, standing against the wall opposite. He had been there all the time.

"Then you do not love me," he said.

"Oh, Taras, I never said I *loved* you. I said that I *liked* you."

"I will not trouble you any more."

"Taras!" I said, moving a step forward and taking his arm as he turned to go. "Come inside, for a minute, please."

"There is nothing to say."

"Please?"

He nodded, reluctantly, and walked into my room before me.

"Please sit down?" I asked him and he obediently sat on the chair. I perched on the edge of the bed and decided to lie:

"I do like you, very much, but I have somebody else back in England."

"Do you love him?"

"I don't know," I replied carefully, feeling that this was rather a good way of explaining my reluctance to get involved with Taras. I continued with the deception, telling myself that it was to spare his feelings: "I'm having trouble deciding who I would rather be with; you or him. I couldn't let you in here before because I didn't think it fair."

"Why?"

"Because if I let you in we might start kissing again."

"I wouldn't mind."

"No, nor would I. But it wouldn't have been fair on this other boy."

"I don't care about him."

I laughed at his honesty and he smiled back nervously.

"I like kissing you," he said. "But we don't have to go any further than that."

"What do you mean?" I asked, genuinely not considering that there might have been any further to go.

"I wasn't planning to sleep with you."

"Oh!"

I was taken aback by his abruptness. And then, I admit, a very stupid feeling came over me. My pride was hurt at the thought that this young man who had said that he loved me did not want to go to bed with me. It was a stupid reaction, I know.

He stood up and smiled down at me.

"How long do you need to decide between us?"

"I don't know."

"I will wait for you."

I took his hand because I suddenly thought that I was going to be alone again. My story was a fabrication;

there was nobody else in England. If there had been then perhaps I could have endured my loneliness there in the Ukraine. Taras offered some comfort.

He ran his hand through my hair and said, "You are confused."

"I am," I conceded, glad that this was the truth, even if I was wilfully misunderstanding him. I stood and faced him.

"I will try and help you decide," he said and kissed me. And I decided to stop analysing the situation I found myself in.

A few evenings later, a Sunday, Taras took me to a party somewhere on the outskirts of the city. It was in a large but run-down house and although very few people there were students, they were all of his age. The music was heavy but tuneful in a meandering, aimless sort of way and everyone had to talk loudly to be heard above it.

It was very dark in all of the rooms, and crowded, and I became bored quite quickly because I could not easily join in with any of the conversations. Taras was considerate, though, and unselfishly acted as translator for me some of the time, but the talk was a little tedious. When people discovered that I was English they often wanted to ask me about well-known English celebrities because they were easy references. I had answered the same questions so many times before that it was with some relief that I found Taras was tiring of it all as well. He took me to a corner of a room at the back of the house that was even darker still and perhaps just a little bit quieter. Here we kissed, and in the gloom where we could not be seen I let him slip his hand up my shirt and massage my breast. I did try to push his hand away but without any conviction and I admit that I was enjoying myself as much as he was.

However, I then tried putting my hand into his trousers and he pushed me away.

"No, not that!" he said, serious.

"I'm sorry," I replied. I pushed back his floppy hair and kissed his ear. "But you excite me. I would like to make love with you."

"I know, but I don't want to, yet. I don't know you well enough."

And now I felt a complete fool; cheap. I hadn't thought that he would still feel like that.

"I understand," I said, annoyed, and we decided to leave, walking back to the Hall, hand in hand, but making little conversation. It was a lovely night, if a little chilly, but neither of us said what we really felt. When we were back in our corridor we kissed, pretending that everything was all right between us, and went to our separate rooms.

And I slept badly. My earplugs never quite muffled the sounds of the other students returning late, and noisily, to their rooms, and somebody in another corridor appeared to be having a party of their own. Everything combined to make me feel even more irritable and serious about leaving for home.

However, the following week I was too busy to worry about my problems. On the Monday my tutor suddenly announced that he was going to Kiev for two days and could take me along with him to see a couple of Alexander de Saussure's recent buildings. I just had time to return to the Hall to pack a few things, return to the School of Architecture, and leave with him in his very old Mercedes. I didn't have time to tell anyone that I was going, but Taras was the only person who might have been interested in my movements. I didn't leave him a note, and felt bad about this the whole time that I was away. The trip is a story in itself but I will make it brief.

Visiting Kiev went well enough and I was impressed both by the city and de Saussure's buildings. Unfortunately the car broke down on our return and we spent an unplanned couple of days in Uman. The car, we were constantly assured, would be repaired at any moment, but the hours, then the days dragged on. We stayed in a small hotel and my tutor insisted that he would pay for everything because I was only a poor student and the problems with the car were his fault because he had not maintained it properly.

On the first day there we went to a park and sitting on a bench he took hold of my hand and kissed it. I was horrified that he was about to proposition me and that he had engineered the whole situation. I was being rather self-centred, however, for what he wanted to confide was that he was homosexual and was considering leaving his wife and family for another tutor at the University. I don't know that I was able to give him any useful advice, but I listened to him dutifully and as compassionately as I could. It was a stressful couple of days.

Upon my return to Odessa I found a letter waiting for me in the Department saying that Alexander de Saussure would be pleased to meet me for an interview at his office that evening in the city centre. It was dated three days previously. I barely had time to grab my research notes and borrow a Dictaphone, and I arrived a half-hour late and out of breath.

De Saussure's offices were in an elegant Victorian building of classical proportions and detailing, but the interior had been gutted to create a thoroughly modern set of working spaces. I was shown into a conference room, immediately dropped my notes, and despaired of making a good impression. However, to my surprise it went well. De Saussure was amused that I was so evidently flustered, and with good humour he showed me how to operate the Dictaphone.

I felt untidy, ill-prepared and out of place, but for two hours he was happy to explain his design philosophy to me as it related to his recent work. Somehow I managed to ask intelligent questions and sounded as if I knew what I was talking about.

De Saussure struck me as handsome; a tall man with greying hair and large hands, he was a charismatic character and I liked him immensely. He made many references to other contemporary architects, to great architects and artists of the past, and provided me with much useful material for my PhD. He re-ignited my enthusiasm not only for his own work but for contemporary architecture in general. I had been unable to see any way forward with my thesis until that meeting, but suddenly I was enthused. De Saussure obviously sensed this and asked me if I would like to return the next day and attend a presentation.

When I returned to the Hall that evening I was worried that Taras might be standing outside of my door, but despite the fact that I had managed to leave the lights on in my room he was not there waiting. I reined in my ego and worked late into the night, rising early the next morning to walk into the Department and transcribe the interview of the previous day directly onto a word processor. I hadn't finished at lunchtime when I had to stop to go back to the offices of Alexander de Saussure for the presentation.

Once again I was shown into the conference room where one of the architects explained that this was not to be a presentation to a client but to other professionals, engineers, etc., who would be working on the design if it all went ahead. The following week, he explained, the same kind of presentation was scheduled for the clients, and then it would all be repeated for the planners.

Alexander de Saussure was obviously comfortable before an audience and enjoyed presenting his new design for a development on a cliff-side some distance along the coast from Odessa. I could not understand much of what he said but the model he unveiled suggested that if it could be built then more awards would soon be forthcoming. From the north the building was understated and had very little visual impact, being partly underground with an earth roof. However, once a visitor was inside the building the main corridor would widen, brighten, and finally open out to offer a great atrium space with wide views out over the Black Sea. This southern façade, entirely of steel and tinted glass, was to be cantilevered out over the water and would be quite breathtaking.

I made notes and drew sketches, and became so absorbed that when de Saussure later addressed me I didn't immediately realise that I should look up.

"I have explained to my colleagues here that you are studying my work for your PhD," he said, amused at my surprise. "Would you like to give us your opinion of the project?"

"It'll have to be in English," I replied, reluctantly.

"Of course. Most of us will understand."

"Well," I said, putting down my papers and pen as twenty sets of eyes were turned to me. I felt very uncertain of myself. "I assume that the entrance is so modestly designed for environmental reasons, as well as for reasons of theatre. It has a minimal impact on the landscape and conceals what is to be discovered. I like the way that anyone using the building will progress through the earth, as it were, from the small-scale, relatively dark rooms, through to larger, lighter spaces, until the main route ends in the atrium with the curtain-wall of glass and the view out over the sea. To continue the route with the balcony, or half-bridge seems . . . "

He raised his eyebrows, encouraging me to continue, but I could not think of the right word. I decided upon "inevitable" and he nodded, sagely.

"Ideally," he said, "at the end of the bridge the person who has been progressing through the building should be able to throw themselves off and become one with the air, with the elements."

"And from the sea," I added. "Which is not an elevation that many people will witness, it is a startling and bold statement. There is something primitive, or primordial about the entrance, but the progression through to the unashamedly modern part is bold and marvellously handled."

"Thank you," de Saussure replied, evidently appreciating my comments. "Unfortunately I now have to persuade these gentlemen that the earth roof at the entrance to the building can be strong enough for the load, and watertight. And that the curtain wall and cantilevered portions of the building can be built with the delicacy I envision. Engineers, eh?"

I left the presentation very impressed and returned to the Department for a late night writing up my thoughts. I got back to the Hall of Residence some time after midnight and went immediately to my room and got into bed. Somebody was playing loud music close-by so I put in my earplugs and started to read. However, after my busy few days, I fell asleep immediately and awoke the next morning with my light still on and the magazine lying on my chest.

∞

It was a Friday and I got up early, determined to go back into the Department to write up my notes. My mind was full of questions that I wanted to ask de Saussure and I decided to put them into a letter, if only to get them into some coherent order. I jotted a couple of things down while I dressed, and then went to leave. I had been so wrapped up in my thoughts that Taras standing outside my door made me jump.

"So, you *are* in there," he said simply. He looked tired, his eyes dark-shadowed. He was wearing a tee shirt and jeans that looked a little crumpled.

"Yes. You weren't waiting for me, were you?"

"You were pretending that you were not in."

"No," I insisted, making the adjustment from being absorbed by architectural matters, to considering Taras, who I had not really thought about for almost a week. "I use earplugs at night."

"Is that so you can ignore my knocking?"

My heart sank. I asked him back into my room but he would not sit down. He looked about him, distracted and sad, waiting for an explanation. I apologised for not telling him what I had been doing, and related the hectic events of the last few days.

"Those are all good excuses," he said simply. "You have had a long time to think of them. But I know the real reason you are ignoring me."

"What's that?"

"Because I wouldn't sleep with you."

I grinned, which was thoughtless of me and he seemed to take it badly. I was horrified that over the last few days, while I had been preoccupied, Taras might have worked himself into a state over our creaky relationship. How often had he come and knocked on my door, convinced that I was inside but hiding from him? Usually, I would have been elsewhere, but perhaps at other times I had actually been inside, but sound asleep with my earplugs in.

"Taras. I have been thoughtless . . . " I started to say, but he leant over and put his finger to my lips.

"If this is all I need to do to have you, then I give myself to you," he said, and started to take off his t-shirt.

"No, Taras," I protested, but was unable to stop him removing it and letting it drop to the ground. He then started to unbuckle his belt and I decided that I had to take control of what was happening.

I grabbed his hands to stop him.

"You don't have to do this," I said firmly. "I respect you too much, and like you too much, and yes, I'd like to sleep with you, but not like this."

"I don't mind," he insisted. "There's nothing that I wouldn't do for you."

"Put your shirt back on," I said, as levelly as I could.

He bent down and picked it up, holding it to his skinny chest.

"Do you love me?" he asked.

"Yes," I replied, desperate for him to get dressed and out of my room. The whole scene annoyed me, and he annoyed me, although I knew that it was entirely my fault. "Yes, I love you. But please get dressed." It seemed the easiest thing to say.

He put his shirt back on, gloomily, deliberately.

"Why have you been hiding for the last few days?"

"I haven't," I repeated, tired and frustrated. "I've been working. Look, how about we go out tonight?"

He smiled at this and I told him to be ready at seven o'clock. I insisted, though, that at that moment I had to go back into the Department.

As I walked into the city centre and the School of Architecture my thoughts were at first of the mess that I had created with Taras. I was annoyed that I had told him I loved him, and that I had agreed to meet him later that day. Perhaps, by that evening, I might have been in a more receptive mood for his company, but my thesis was rather more important to me at that moment and by the time I arrived at the Department it was once again uppermost in my thoughts. I share a small room there with another, harder-working postgraduate student, but that morning he was not in. With the place to myself I spread out my papers on both his desk and mine and started to see how my thesis might take shape. At any other time I would have wasted half of the morning walking down to the office to see if there was any mail for me, going to the coffee machine, and even wandering into the studios to see what the other students were up to, but that day I set immediately to work. I could see how the PhD could be divided up into a number of distinct sections, each having a separate building as a case study, and I put my notes in piles with photographs, drawings and copies of magazine articles. Just doing this brought ideas to mind, associations and themes that I would want to explore. I made notes of these before they slipped from my mind, and wrote down references to the work of other architects that I would need to follow up. It was exciting to realise just how much of my thesis could be written with the aid of my interview with de Saussure, but slightly worrying that I would need to do so much extra research to back up what he had told me.

Once it all seemed to make sense I rationalised my piles of papers and turned on the word processor to start transcribing the rest of the interview from the Dictaphone.

While I was waiting for it to boot up my supervising tutor put his head around the door and coughed, startling me.

"I'm sorry," he apologised.

"I didn't hear you coming."

"I have just had a telephone call from Alexander de Saussure," he informed me. "He asked whether it would be right for him to offer you a position in his company?"

"A job? Doing what?"

"He called it 'International Public Relations'."

"Goodness! Really?"

"Yes. He telephoned to discuss whether it was . . . " he struggled for the word, " . . . ethical, to offer you the position. He doesn't want it to conflict with your studies."

"It won't, will it?"

"It might. But as long as you put plenty of hours into your PhD, you could be in a better position for research if you are working for him."

"I don't know what to say."

He shrugged. "You will have to talk to him," was all that he would say before he left.

I waited for the news to sink in, but as it would not I walked down the corridor to my tutor's office and asked if I could telephone de Saussure. He agreed, got me an outside line and held on until the call was through to the architect himself. Then he left.

At some time in the middle of the following night I awoke and remembered Taras. In the pit of my stomach it gave me an unpleasant, hollow feeling. I wondered what on earth I was doing? I had thought that I was in control of everything but suddenly I doubted myself. Quietly snoring beside me was Alexander de Saussure.

In his office the architect had offered me a very good position with an enviable salary and insisted that although

I would have to regularly visit the Ukraine I could work from London. I refused to accept such a proposition immediately, and although he said that this was entirely reasonable he started to joke that he was upset that I couldn't accept there and then. In the same spirit I told him that I was a difficult woman to persuade, and that he would have to try harder. We flirted rather, and to show that I wasn't ungrateful I agreed that he could buy me dinner. It was a silly game, but I didn't want him to think that I would simply accept any offer that he cared to make. What was more, I told him that if he was taking me out it would have to be to an expensive restaurant.

We got on very well while I teased him over what I did or did not think of his offer, and he insisted that if I was to keep him waiting for an answer then there would have to be small forfeits in return. For example, he insisted that I select the wine, and insisted that I choose well, so I simply decided upon a very expensive bottle. When he tried to top up my glass and I demurred, he reminded me that the wine had been my choice and that it was not cheap. When we had finished eating he said that he thought he could persuade me to accept the offer that very night, but we would have to have liqueurs with our coffee so that he could have the time to talk me around.

Next to the restaurant was a hotel with a dark, comfortable bar, and we went there afterwards to continue our conversation. I knew the implications of this and I was happy for the evening to come to its inevitable conclusion.

But at four in the morning, in the hotel room which was too warm and stuffy, though luxuriously appointed, I did not feel so certain of myself. I had no real qualms about who I was sharing a bed with, but I was concerned as to how Taras would feel that I had stood him up. Thoughts of him in that oppressive Hall of Residence went around and around in my thoughts. I lay under a very thin sheet feeling hot and uncomfortable. It took a great mental effort to relax and think of other things before I was able to sleep again.

I returned to the Hall of Residence at some time in the middle of the morning and was pleased that Taras was not hanging around. Somebody, Taras I assumed, had left what looked like a large, sealed jiffy bag outside of my door so I picked it up and let myself in. Although I had showered at the hotel I was still in my clothes from the day before and I was about to change them when I casually examined the contents of the parcel that had been left for me.

The bag looked new but it was stained an unpleasant brown at the bottom. I tore it open and tried to tip the contents out onto my desk but they seemed to be stuck. Looking in I could see something dark and felt instinctively that shaking it vigorously was preferable to putting my hand inside. What fell on the desk with a thump appeared to be a large lump of old meat, bloody, gristly and fatty and starting to dry up. I dropped the bag and backed away, appalled that somebody could have left such a thing for me. I couldn't believe that Taras had done it.

It took me several moments to compose myself. I found an old plastic bag and with a ruler I pushed the thing lying on my desk into the bag. I felt nauseous at the pressure I had to use to move the weight of the lump of old meat, and at the extra effort required because it had slightly adhered to the desk. When it fell into the plastic bag the sudden weight of it made me feel shaky and I dropped it and jumped back, unable to stop the stupid reaction. Gingerly, and without looking into the plastic bag, I then put the stained jiffy bag inside as well.

I washed my hands in the sink and then wiped down my desk and threw the soiled tissues into the bag, which I then tied up. I detested the thought that by carrying the bag up the corridor I was somehow associated with whatever it was that I couldn't identify. When I dropped it into the large dustbin outside I felt so much happier, although I returned to my room with some hesitation, worried that there might be something else to confront.

The damp patch on my desk had dried by the time that I had changed my clothes, and although I wasn't sure that I was in the mood for work, I decided to go back to the Architecture Department. I certainly didn't want to stay around in the Hall, and I was desperate to tell somebody who might appreciate the news about my job offer of the previous day. I was still shaken and angry, but as I walked out of the grounds I was already thinking about what had happened between myself and Alexander de Saussure, and wishing that I had some close girlfriend to whom I could confide.

As I reached the gate into the street Taras appeared before me. He walked directly out in front of me and I stopped, my heart thumping.

"Did you find it?" he asked quietly. He looked terribly ill.

"So it was you," I said, appalled, but unable to think of anything other than his terrible appearance. He was unnaturally pale, his skin almost translucent, and this was emphasised by his stubble and his dark-shadowed eyes. He was wearing an old, stained coat, which he had pulled exaggeratedly tight about him with dirty hands.

"What the hell was it?" I asked, but as I did so I suddenly thought that I knew.

"It was for you," he said, his words pained and awkward.

℥

Nina Monkman stopped her narrative and stared down into her glass of wine as if to find something there to replace what she could see in her memory.

"You are going to think me mad . . ."

"Are you suggesting . . . ?" I started to ask and she nodded vigorously.

"A prank," she said determinedly. "It was a trick, a horribly cruel trick. He had every reason to be angry with me, but why so nasty? Why so macabre? He pulled open his coat and his shirt and his trousers were completely sodden with what appeared to be blood."

"What did you do?"

"I did what any other self-respecting woman would do, of course. I had hysterics and ran."

"Where?"

"Away, from him. I don't quite know where I went, probably only two or three streets away, and then I calmed down a little, and went back to Alexander. He must have wondered what kind of madwoman he had been with the previous night, but he listened to what I said and we went to the police, and then they listened patiently to what I had to say."

"And what did you say?"

"Only what I told you . . . I told them what happened. I said that it could only have been a sick trick but they asked me what I thought Taras had meant to suggest. I couldn't say it, though."

"And what did the police find?"

"That Taras was missing. In the dustbin they found the bag, with his blood on it, but nothing inside. There were still traces of blood on my desk, but in his room it was everywhere."

"What do they think happened?"

"They don't know and they won't say. But they asked me so many questions, and they didn't want me coming back to England for Christmas. They want to ask me more questions when I return next week."

"Are you going back?"

"I think I have to. I have to know for sure that it was all a horrible joke."

In Hiding

For the first time since his arrival in Arkos the Right Honourable David Barrett, M.P. was up early, washed and dressed and standing on the quay. Behind him the town seemed angular, dusty and harsh, but the sun was bright and glittered off the sea. In the distance the island of Elga looked green, fresh and inviting.

There were a number of fishermen about at that hour, stretching out their nets to dry and talking with good humour amongst themselves. They didn't seem to mind him staring at them, trying to fathom their actions. At least Barrett had now seen them with their boats: it had appeared unlikely that their craft were intended to be purely picturesque.

It was cool enough to stand in the sun and enjoy its warmth without discomfort, and the Englishman felt it on his face as he closed his eyes. When he opened them again it was to see a boat approaching from the island.

A man in a red shirt sat in the back of the small craft by the outboard motor, the sound of which reached Barrett a few moments later and increased in volume as he came into the harbour. Barrett assumed that this must be Simon. There was nowhere obvious for him to tie up though, so the pilot of the boat pointed to a small wooden jetty a short distance away and turned in that direction.

Barrett walked over to meet him, stepping over the paraphernalia of the fishermen, watching as the man cut the engine just before the jetty, and let the boat continue under its own momentum. He was not intending to stop, however, and as the boat came alongside Barrett, he motioned for the English M.P. to jump aboard while it was close enough. It rocked and lurched as the man stepped in, and immediately the pilot pulled at the engine and it started up again. Barrett marvelled that anyone could appear to be so at ease on the water, moving about the boat gracefully, turning it and giving the engine full throttle once he had it aimed back in the direction of the open sea. His passenger sat towards the front and once he had composed himself he enjoyed the slight breeze and the sprays of water that came over the side from time to time.

"I assume that you're taking me to see Taylor?" he shouted over the noise of the engine.

The young man smiled, apparently in agreement, and Barrett told himself to relax. Even if this man wasn't Simon and didn't speak a word of English, what did it matter? He had become so tired of his predicament that he no longer cared what risks he took. What could be worse than the calamities that had so recently befallen him?

The boat left the harbour, passing a couple of birds which Barrett assumed were gulls; they seemed unconcerned at both the boat and the small wake that made them bob up and down. Barrett could see further up the mainland as Arkos shrank behind them, and noticed that Taylor's island was still quite sheltered, despite being a half mile out at sea. Along the coastline to the north there appeared to be army buildings of some kind, but they may well have been older fortifications. They were too far away for him to be able to see whether they were still in use. To the south the coastline looked a little gentler, though still rocky. The tourist beaches were at least a couple of dozen miles further away with their stretches of inviting sand.

The island of Elga grew closer, and through the dark green of the trees Barrett could make out two houses. They were both built of the dull yellow local stone, but one looked run-down and perhaps burnt-out. Then the sun reflected off something brightly and was immediately gone again.

The boat soon started to skirt the island and they made for what Barrett now saw to be a very small harbour with one other similar boat in it. The engine was cut, as before, and they coasted in and alongside a low concrete arm in which were set rusty iron steps. The young man deftly took the rope and climbed up, pulling it through an iron ring. The boat stopped with a jerk and was then secured against the wall. The sea here was clear, unlike the harbour at Arkos, and Barrett could see the sand a few feet below him. Fish darted past and apparently out into the wide water of the Mediterranean.

He stood uncertainly and climbed up after the pilot, who turned and offered him a hand.

"Welcome to Elga," said the young man with an unmistakeable northern English accent.

"Thank you."

Just ahead of them was one of the houses.

"You're expected up there," Simon suggested, but Barrett took his time to look out to sea, wondering if he could make out a coast on the far horizon. It was strange to be on an inland sea; having been brought up on the south coast of England he had always assumed that such stretches of water went on forever, getting colder and wilder. But this was enclosed, safe-seeming.

Barrett turned back to the house; it was magnificently situated. A series of stone terraces led up from the harbour to its whitewashed walls. Trees pressed all around this side of the island, but Barrett could see that they thinned further around, allowing views to the north. It seemed so much cooler there than in the town. There was a breeze blowing, and the stone balustrade, when he touched it as he ascended the last few steps up to the house, was still cold. There was vegetation everywhere, with brightly coloured flowers. And there were lizards, motionless, willing the sun to burn with more heat. Next to him, in the grass, a cicada shrilled, and high above in the blue vault a bird called.

Taylor appeared, standing on the top step in front of the house.

"Welcome to my domain," he said with a broad smile on his great, square face.

Only two days previously Barrett had booked himself into a Spartan hotel in the small, dusty Greek port that the guidebook had insisted had little to commend it to the casual tourist. He had arrived in darkness, and it was without great hopes that he had drawn back the curtains on his first morning. He had no idea of what to expect and, frankly, it could have been worse. There was a small bay with boats in the harbour, but the buildings were too modern to be attractive, and perhaps the boats were too functional to really be pleasing to the eye. He had been woken early by the sound of the cars and scooters under his window, the noise of which echoed around the semi-circular port long after they had passed out of it.

At that moment he tried not to think of why he had ended up in Arkos, but, unbidden, recent memories of his wife's face, the Prime Minister's anger, and the newspaper reporter's obvious enjoyment of his plight rose up before him. He had been able to face up to the scandal for only so long. When his Party had publicly chastised him he still had the support of his wife, but when she decided that she should distance herself from him, then it had all become too much to bear. Friends slipped away from him, becoming mysteriously unavailable, and his family suddenly found it impractical to see him. For almost a week, when he thought that he had the support of those around him, he had been able to ignore the fact that he really had made a career-ending mistake.

On his first morning in Arkos he borrowed the guidebook from the hotel lobby and read about the local archaeology. He thought that perhaps he should try to see it, but he found life much more relaxing if he simply sat in the little café in the middle of the harbour and watched the world pass by before him.

The café was dark but bustling and he had formed the notion that he would sit there and write. Despite all that went on around him, he was trying to explain on paper the set of circumstances that had allowed him to appear to pocket the old lady's half a million pounds. It was a technical argument, and one that he felt he should be able to defend. On the first afternoon, though, he had started to lose interest, and he ended up playing draughts with an old fisherman who came in to drink retsina. The language barrier meant that they could not talk and that suited Barrett.

It was at the end of his second day in the café, when he had all but abandoned writing, as the sun was setting splendidly over the sea, that a man was suddenly at his shoulder.

"Hello there. Barrett, isn't it?"

He looked up and saw a very tall man; he was large in that way that denoted aristocratic blood. Barrett was only a Socialist for the sake of his political career, but he had never liked this kind of person with a booming voice, air of confidence and expansive gestures. He was over-sized, he assumed, because generations of his family had been well-fed at the expense of ordinary people.

"Yes," he agreed, reluctantly. "I'm David Barrett." He had already decided that if challenged he might as well reveal his identity.

"I'm Taylor, Ferdinand Taylor. You remember? We met at Hugh Golightly's party, after the Derby, oh, twelve years ago?"

Barrett stood up reluctantly and had his hand engulfed in Taylor's. It was squeezed mercilessly.

"Twelve years, is it?" asked Barrett, who was not sure if he recognised the man.

"I'm afraid so. I've been here for ten years, you know. Rarely see a pale English face. So why are you in Arkos?"

"Don't ask!"

"Oh, like that, is it?"

Barrett nodded and offered the man the chair opposite.

"How is old Golightly?" the man asked.

"Oh, you know, still stinking rich."

"Still able to lose a fortune on the horses each year without ever touching his capital, eh?"

"I'm surprised you remember me."

"Oh, I had years working as a journalist. Trained myself to remember faces and facts, gossip and indiscretion."

He looked pleased with himself, but was concerned at his companion's hang-dog expression.

"What's up, old man?"

"I just can't believe my bad luck, that's all."

"I'll try not to take that personally."

"Well, I've come all the way here to the middle of nowhere to escape the British press, and who do I bump into? Only a bloody journalist!"

"I've retired, dear fellow, I've retired."

"But do you chaps ever hang up your notebook? Isn't it worth a few thousand quid for you to phone your old paper and cry, 'Hold the front page! David Barrett's in hiding in Greece'?"

"No, not anymore. I left England under a cloud myself. But what have you done, old fellow, what have you done? If your whereabouts is worth that much money . . . ?"

"You really haven't heard?"

"No. There're no British papers to be had here. So, have you been caught shagging your secretary?"

"No. It's financial . . . "

"No need to justify yourself to me. I'm well out of that game."

"I'm not sure that I believe you."

"I'll come clean. Ten years ago a certain newspaper editor was discovered to have had a gay affair, despite the anti-homosexual rants in his newspaper . . . "

"It sounds vaguely familiar."

"Well, I was the one who sold the story to his rival newspaper."

"I hope you were well paid?"

"Handsomely. But then, I had to be. Because *I* was his lover."

"Really?"

"Yes. And they had to pay enough to make it worthwhile that I was a part of the story. And they did. And I have taken an early retirement . . . here."

"In Arkos?"

"No, not quite. I have a small island just out there," he waved his hand in the general direction of the sea. "It's called Elga."

"But why here? Because it's remote?"

"Well, an old school chum owned it and was talking of selling-up. When I looked into it I was impressed that

I could afford a whole island. Arkos itself was dismissed in the particulars as a 'small and friendly port where hotels overlook the boats and the nets of the fishermen'." He waved out of the café window in confirmation.

"So, do you want to know the details of my disgrace?" asked Barrett, feeling that perhaps, after all, he would like to justify himself to somebody who might listen without having been prejudiced by the rabid newspapers.

"Tomorrow. Tell me tomorrow. You come over very early and I'll show you around my island. And we'll swim, and have lunch, and then maybe, only maybe, we'll drink enough retsina for me to be bothered with your story," he smiled again. "But if I can drag you away from whatever you're writing, you must tell me what you've been up to while you've been here. Where are you staying? The hotel at the end?"

"Yes, I didn't think there was much choice?"

"No. Simon's family stayed there sometimes when they used to visit. When did you arrive?"

"Only two days ago. I read about the archaeology. I've been meaning to look for the ruins; there was once meant to have been an Oracle at Arkos."

"Most of the remains have long gone. The port's been developed over the centuries. There're some old building on the hillside above us. There're a few bits and pieces on Elga, but nothing of significance."

There was an awkward pause. Barrett knew that he should be asking Taylor about himself but he could not quite bring himself to.

"So, have you burnt all of your bridges, then?" Taylor asked, at length.

"I didn't think you wanted to know the details until tomorrow?"

"I don't. I was just wondering whether you were planning on going back at some time and trying to salvage your life.

You never know; people do bounce back, if they've got the strength, and arrogance. Or are you intending to spend the rest of your life in this hole?"

"I suppose I intend to go back some time. Perhaps when all this blows over, and I'm no longer in the news."

"Wife and children?"

"Wife. No children."

"Well. Perhaps we'll talk properly tomorrow?"

Taylor stood up and took Barrett's hand once more:

"Tomorrow. I'll send the boat for you, at about nine."

And with that he turned and left.

Barrett was dumbfounded. He finished his drink, picked up his papers and walked back to the hotel, its presence announced by an illuminated sign on the dusty roadside. It was a small establishment, although it echoed disconcertingly like a grand palace.

His room was small and sparsely furnished but it had a balcony. The hotel stood at one end of the harbour, facing the buildings on the other side of the bay, but he could still peer out to sea and to the island he guessed was Elga; it was a dark shape against the light evening sky. Barrett stared at it for a long time from the balcony while the frequency of the cars lessened on the road underneath his vantage point, and after a while only the occasional scooters and motorbikes buzzed loudly below him. He was waiting for lights to shine on Elga, but they didn't appear.

※

The island seemed to be very lush compared to the mainland, although the little terraces that stepped back down from the house to the edge of the sea were overgrown with pale, dry grass. They were probably old, abandoned fields. Barrett could see one of the old wartime buildings through the trees near to them and tried to remember which army might have built it. The air was alive with the sounds of insects.

He followed Taylor around the side of the house and he could see that it was bigger than it had at first appeared, being ranged around an open courtyard, overlooking the terraces and out to sea. Several of the windows were shuttered, but there was one large glazed opening in the middle of the collection of buildings.

"There are good stone slabs under this," Taylor kicked at the pale grass that covered the yard; it was thick, sharp stuff, interwoven with straying creepers and brambles. "The fountain's never worked," he said as Barrett was trying to understand the arrangement of stone and rusted metal in front of them.

On the far side there was a barn and a couple of cart-sized entrances, and Barrett expected to see a few chickens. No part of the building was particularly interesting from any architectural point of view, but with its clay tiles and small windows it made a pleasing composition. He noticed that Simon was no longer with them.

Taylor led him inside, where it was dark and cooler still. Once his eyes had become accustomed to the gloom he could see that it was very tastefully converted. The stone flags in the kitchen were highly polished, and the big bare table in the centre looked newly scrubbed. It was well and expensively appointed, and from a large stainless steel refrigerator Taylor produced two large bottles of beer and opened them. He sat at the table and placed one of the glasses in the place opposite him, inviting Barrett to sit there. They looked out through the large, glazed doorway.

"You look well," Taylor said, pouring his beer. The words were considered, measured.

"I feel better," replied Barrett, doing the same. "I hoped I'd left all my troubles miles behind me, in England, but in Arkos it didn't really feel like that. But here, now, on your island, it's different."

"I understand. It's special here. It seems like so long ago that I escaped from my own past. But go on, tell me, what occurred back in 'Blighty' that drove you here. You might as well unburden yourself, man!"

"The short version of events," Barrett explained, "is that about twenty years ago, starting out as a solicitor, I had the dubious honour of acting as Executor for an awkward old lady. Her financial affairs were so incredibly convoluted and slipshod that just about all of her estate would've disappeared into legal fees if I hadn't taken a few short cuts. One of the main liberties that I took was with regard to some assets that should have been transferred to a very questionable evangelist church. They appeared to have several ministers and no congregation, and two of the ministers were convicted criminals. It didn't trouble my conscience that I was able to acquire the assets myself for a very advantageous sum. It was completely wrong legally, but morally? Well, I didn't think they should get the money."

"But it's come back to haunt you?"

"Yes. They church had known for some years what I'd done, but were waiting for the moment to use the information to their advantage. I was about to be promoted to the Cabinet and they tried blackmailing me. I refused to go along with their demands so they told the newspapers about my activities twenty years earlier."

"And the newspapers have torn you to pieces?"

"They wouldn't have been so interested in me if I hadn't recently been arguing for more controls on the Press."

"Do you consider yourself unlucky?"

"Yes! Exactly. What I did was wrong, but it still doesn't trouble my conscience. It is simply bad luck that it came out. I just wish, right now, that I had the resources to buy myself an island. This looks like paradise to me."

Taylor sipped his beer, staring out the window, and Barrett took the opportunity to do the same.

"It's not quite paradise," the host said, slowly. "It should've been."

"I've told you my woes . . . " Barrett invited him.

"I didn't invite you here so that I could tell you mine, though."

"It only seems fair."

"I suppose it always helps to hear of somebody else's misfortunes. It wouldn't hurt to have some one else to sympathise . . . not that I expect that to ease the pain."

"But if it is painful, you don't have to."

"It was once unbearable, but the years pass . . . I wake up every day here in 'paradise', but immediately I remember what happened and it's all spoilt for me."

He sipped his beer once more.

"You see, I met Simon in Arkos one day, about seven or eight years ago, much as I met you. He was on holiday, and I wanted company, and I invited him over here to Elga. And he never left."

"He seems like a nice chap," Barrett said, by way of filling the gap, but was surprised to see Taylor's expression.

"So, you saw him?"

"Of course, when he brought me over."

"He brought you here in the boat?"

"As you arranged, yes. As I said, he seems nice."

He looked aghast:

"But Simon died, just over three years ago. There was a fire, and it was my fault."

"So who was the young man in the boat?"

"There was no young man."

"But who piloted the boat? I didn't do it myself?"

Taylor looked at the surface of the table and simply shook his head.

"So you've seen him too," he mumbled quietly.

"He's not a ghost."

"No? Are you sure of that? Are you very sure?"

"I'm certain. But, look, what is this? I mean, you told me you would send him across to pick me up from Arkos."

"Did I?"

"Yes, hang it all! If this is some attempt at a practical joke . . . "

"No, I assure you," he said, looking back up and searching for something in Barrett's face. The gaze made the man uncomfortable; his host was in earnest.

Barrett suggested:

"Let me go and fetch him in. The man out there who collected me is very real; flesh and blood."

"If you like," replied Taylor calmly, as though convinced that Barrett would be unable to do so.

He got up from the table and, leaving his beer behind him, he walked out into the bright light of the Greek morning. Simon was not in sight, and might take some finding, Barrett realised, but it was not a large island, and the first thing he would do was go back down to the boats to make sure that there were still two tied up there. Before he could get there, though, the young man in the red shirt appeared over to his left with a wheelbarrow full of logs. As he appeared to be coming in Barrett's direction he simply stopped and waited for him.

"Hello again," the visitor said when the man drew close. "This might sound odd, but can I ask you a couple of questions?"

"About Ferdinand? I thought so. I hung around because I knew that something might happen."

"You do realise that he thinks you don't exist?"

"I know. He thinks I'm a ghost," said the young man with a grin. "Perhaps I'd better explain."

He sat on the cool stone balustrade to the steps and said, in a business-like fashion:

"A few years ago there was a fire. It started off as a bonfire. It got out of control. When Ferdinand bought this place there were two houses and both were fully furnished. He emptied the contents of the main house into the second and then moved his own stuff in to the first. And then when I moved here I brought a lot of my own possessions, and we stored the surplus we didn't need in the second house. Then we had a hare-brained scheme to rent out the second house and so had an enormous bonfire to dispose of all the rubbish we'd accumulated. We'd been drinking because it was so hot, and we'd thrown more and more rubbish on the fire. But it was too close to the house, and eventually the whole building went up as well. He got the idea in his head that I was trapped in the burning house when all I'd done was go down to the shore to try and fill up some buckets with water."

"He thought you'd died?" asked Barrett.

"Yes, poor old Ferdinand. Wouldn't be budged from the idea, even when I turned up safe and well."

"That must have been awful for him."

"Yes, for the both of us. He had a breakdown. I don't know if you've ever tried reasoning with someone who is in such a state. It was as though he didn't recognise me. Well, he had to be hospitalised. And he was in and out for five or six years while they tried to find the right balance of drugs. But to ease his psychosis the drugs they gave him made him physically ill. We tried so many combinations, and each had to be left for months to settle down to see if they'd have the desired long term effect."

"That must have been awful."

"It wasn't good. But his family came over and stayed and were very supportive. And then about two years ago, when he was very ill again, we decided to remove all of his medication. Within weeks he was fit and well, almost entirely restored to his old self. The doctors were surprised, but it worked. The only problem was that he still had the idea that I'd died in the fire, and that it was his fault. We decided, me and the family, that in all other respects he was so much better. And as it had been so long since the fire, his grief seemed almost bearable to him. So we simply left everything like that."

"And he thinks that he sees your ghost?"

"His family look after his financial affairs and I'm paid to stay here and look after him. I cook for us, clean, look after the place. And he simply thinks that he's haunted."

"You're a pretty substantial ghost!"

"I should say so!"

"But what should I do? Go back to him and act like everything's normal?"

"Everything *is* normal, apart from his one strange belief. Yes, go back, talk about England and old friends."

"But that's wrong, surely."

"In what way?"

"Morally. I mean, the man may be deluded, but you're colluding with that delusion, reinforcing it."

"What should I do? Go back to experimenting with different doses of drugs? Let them fry his brains with ECT again?"

"They don't do that in this modern age. Go back to Britain rather than stay in this ratty old country . . . Go private . . . See some specialists . . . "

Simon was obviously annoyed and was choosing the words for his reply with care.

"Thank you for your advice, but with all due respect, you don't know what you're talking about. The medical care in this country is just as good as in the UK. And we did go private, although it offered nothing that all the alternatives didn't, except a larger bill. And yes, for your information, even in this enlightened age they do still resort to electrocuting patients because, barbaric as it seems, it can have positive effects."

"I'm sorry, I was only trying to help," Barrett defended himself.

"No. Real 'help' means being here when he is going through sheer physical and mental hell and can't even feed himself. 'Help' is spending the whole day trying to get a very big, uncooperative and belligerent man into a bath because he stinks so badly but doesn't notice. And then when he's in the bath you don't only have to wash him but you have to hold him up so that he doesn't simply slip under the water and drown. Because he's so confused and unable to do anything for himself . . . "

"Okay, okay," Barrett backed away. "Point taken."

"The state he's in at the moment is as close to normal as you could imagine. And it's a blessing."

"I'll go back and pretend I didn't see you."

"You do that," Simon said, almost with a threat in his voice.

Feeling rather aggrieved Barrett walked back to the house. Taylor was in the kitchen and appeared to be preparing food, although it was still quite early.

"We shall have a picnic," he declared. "I'll show you around my island first, by which time we'll have worked up an appetite.

"I'd like that. You can point out the archaeology."

"There's very little left," he explained as they started around the shoreline, travelling clockwise. "The army were here in the Second World War and destroyed most of it. They built the little harbour, and there are a few old pill-boxes, and other horrible things in concrete."

Neither of them said anything as they passed around the second house, lacking its roof and the inside blackened and empty. The holes for its windows were like sightless eyes and seemed to watch them, reproachfully, as they passed by.

"Is there anything you miss about England," Barrett asked Taylor.

"I suppose so, but they're not realistic things."

"What do you mean?"

"If I lived there I'd still want to be in a house in the middle of nowhere, without a telephone or television. Just like here."

"Are you completely cut off from the world outside?"

"I've got a radio, and sometimes I listen to the World Service, but that isn't a realistic picture of what's going on, is it? I think back to my childhood with fondness, and if I returned I'd expect unreasonably endless sunny days in the house I grew up in. But they weren't endlessly sunny, were they?"

"No. It still rains quite a lot."

"I suppose so," he agreed. "But after a few years here I even started to imagine that everyone wears bowler hats and drives Triumph Heralds. I think of men drinking warm ale in coaching inns, and women in flowery dresses in gardens full of night-scented stock . . . "

"Do you miss the people?"

"Not really. There are good people and bad people wherever you go. Mostly good people. There are as many interesting and as many dull people here in Greece as there are in England."

"But you think of England nostalgically?"

"When I'm in a good mood, I suppose so. When I'm well, and happy, I remember the great times, and the stupidity and fun of my old job. But when I'm down I remember the bad times, and the depths to which I descended just to get a story to fill up a few column inches."

Taylor stopped walking. They were at the northernmost point of the island and he was staring out to sea, his eyes searching the horizon for something. In two places Barrett had noticed small areas of sandy beach, but the rest was rocks. They continued their walk, and when they had almost circumnavigated the entire island they cooled their feet in a large stony pool. Taylor insisted that they eat their food looking out to sea rather than back to the mainland, so on a large flat rock he spread out the cloth in which he had wrapped the bread, feta, tomatoes and ham. In a string bag they had carried two bottles of wine and two glasses, but one had broken. Taylor was saying that he couldn't be bothered to go back to the house for another when, in the distance, Barrett saw Simon. His red shirt was unmistakable, and now that he had started to saw up logs they could also hear him.

Taylor noticed that something had caught Barrett's attention and turned as well, and so Barrett looked down at the food and broke off a piece of bread. He scraped some feta on to it and looked at it carefully, not wanting to know whether Taylor was looking at Simon.

"So, you can see him as well?"

"Yes," Barrett admitted.

"Good," he said, with a certain finality. "I told them I didn't want any more of their pills. I told them I was perfectly sane."

"I don't think that discussing it will help."

"You are probably right."

And with that agreement Taylor then went on to regale Barrett with a succession of entertaining stories, many of them quite unbelievable, dating back to his days as a journalist. He was quite unashamed that he had worked in the "tawdry" end of the business, and claimed that all of his best stories were the result of "pillow-talk".

"Not that I had the pleasure of the pillow myself," he said. "We paid young men and women, depending on the tastes of the target, to wheedle their way into the affections of useful people and it was amazing what stories they would tell."

"Wasn't it immoral?"

"But we were usually exposing the immorality of the people we targeted. Let's call it 'amoral'."

After they had finished the second bottle of wine Barrett realised how sleepy he was, with the alcohol and the heat. Taylor talked on, becoming more and more indiscreet, and his listener wished that he had a notebook to take down the stories because some of them were priceless. He desperately hoped that he would remember one about the early career of the current Prime Minister; it might just help if he ever wanted to go back into politics.

Sleep, however, overcame the unfortunate M.P., and Taylor's stories merged with dreams which were inspired by his recent problems back in London and when he awoke he could not disentangle the two in his fuddled mind. He was lying on his back and his bones ached abominably from the rocks he had unwisely chosen for a bed. The skin on his face felt tight and smarting from the sun and he realised he must be burnt. He couldn't work out how long he had been asleep, but Taylor was no longer there. Barrett had not imagined their picnic, though, for the remains of the bread were on the ground beside him, and there was a little wine on his shirtfront.

He stood with great discomfort and looked back at the island. It couldn't be more than ten acres altogether, and though he couldn't see his host, he could make out Simon in his bright shirt walking from the house towards the little harbour. He decided to go after him, believing that now would be a good time to leave, if the young man thought he could do so without appearing rude.

Barrett walked with care over the rough ground and while some distance away Simon turned and saw him coming. He crossed his arms and waited, and when they were close enough he was the first to speak.

"I'm afraid you've rather caught the sun."

"I guessed I had. Taylor left me to sleep. Is my face that red?"

"Very. You're going to peel badly. Ferdinand's having a *siesta* indoors, which is the best place to recover from a liquid lunch," he beamed. "Oh yes, you will peel . . . "

"It's a shame someone didn't wake me. But I was wondering, would it be a good time to leave?"

"If you want to. It doesn't bother me. I'd only end up having to cook for you tonight as well."

"How does Taylor explain the fact that his ghost cooks for him?"

"I'm not sure if he questions it or not," Simon replied, walking back towards the boats. Barrett followed him.

"His mind does use a kind of logic of its own to understand the world, but it's not one that makes sense to anybody else. He lives in an alternative, parallel universe, and we have to respect that."

"But why? There are some objective absolutes; some rights and wrongs we can all agree upon."

"Are there? Are you a Christian? Do you believe in God?"

"Yes, but what's that got to do with it?"

"Well, why is believing in ghosts any more unreasonable than believing that there is a God?"

"Because a belief in God is more of a working hypothesis than a real proposition."

"So you don't believe in God as anything other than a concept? That's fine. But plenty of people believe in God as a very real being. And they think that Christ really was conceived by a virgin, and performed real miracles, and died and yet came back to life. You respect the views of people who claim this as real and true?"

"Of course."

"Well, all that strikes me as a lot more bizarre than Ferdinand's beliefs, even though I can prove to myself that he's mistaken."

At which point they had reached the boat and Simon untied the rope and jumped in, helping Barrett to follow him. Without another word the young man started up the engine and with the sound roaring off the concrete wall he turned the boat and gunned it for the mainland.

Barrett refused to consider the argument that he could not really refute. His head was throbbing abominably and he felt unequal to an intellectual dispute of any kind. He enjoyed the cool air on his face, although the movement of the boat as it sped over the light waves made him feel nauseous. He didn't look back at the island, but resolved that once in his hotel he would have to make a decision as to what to do next. Perhaps a phone call to an old friend would let him know whether the fuss had died down at home. He had a horrible fear that his disappearance might actually have made things worse.

In Arkos Simon stopped the engine before the jetty, as before, and allowed the boat to continue up to it under its own momentum. He didn't allow Barrett more than a second or so to clamber out of the boat, which he somehow managed without falling back into the water. He turned to Simon to thank him for the ride, but the engine was being fired up again, and the young man was already taking the boat back out to sea.

Barrett now felt truly alone for the first time since he had left England. He had been offered a kind of friendship but had refused it. He walked towards his hotel feeling physically and emotionally very tired. When, he asked himself, might his luck start to turn? At the edge of the road he waited for a lorry to pass and a porter from the hotel came up beside him and they crossed together.

"You have caught the sun rather badly?" he said with a tone of voice that was balanced artfully between concern and amusement.

"Yes, I fell asleep outside, in the open."

"And you went to the island?"

"Yes, to visit a fellow countryman."

They were both walking towards the hotel. Barrett did not want the company, he needed the sanctuary of his room as soon as possible.

"You are both from England?"

"Yes. We all are, all three of us."

"All three? But there is only one Englishman on the island."

"The owner, yes, and the man who took me over there in the boat."

"I meant the man in the boat. He lives there alone but he is a bit strange. He talks to ghosts."

"No, you're getting it muddled up. The man who lives on the island thinks that the man in the boat is the ghost."

"No, sir. The man in the boat, I saw him. He lives there alone, although he comes here and says he is looking after many people on the island. The boys go over there sometimes and watch him talking to people only he can see."

They stopped at the door of the hotel and the porter opened it so that Barrett could go in first.

"I think the boys throw stones at him and break his windows sometimes, but he scares them and they don't go there often. Certainly not at night."

Barrett went up to his room and washed and changed, but did not go down for dinner that evening. He sat on his balcony and stared at the island out on the horizon. After the sun had set and darkness crept in from the east, no lights appeared on the island.

Eleanor

David Planer and I walked into the hotel bar through opposite doors and met in the middle of the room before anyone else could accost him. I was able to offer my old friend a drink, which he accepted, almost with alacrity. I commented on his apparent desperation.

"I am a silly old fool," he said, patting his breast pocket. "I have just had a shock. Old men like me should know better. You see, we don't grow any wiser as we get older; there must be a moment in our later middle-age when we start to un-learn everything."

I was not able to immediately reply because I had managed to catch the barman's eye as we had walked over. I put in an order for a pint of best bitter for him, and a vodka and orange for myself, which annoyed a convention delegate in front of me. He turned round and started to complain that he had been waiting to be served long before we had walked up. However, when he saw that I was with David Planer, he smiled and insisted on shaking his hand:

"It's a great privilege to meet you," he insisted.

"If only it was," David replied, sorrowfully. He was possibly the oldest person at the convention, and looked rather out of place in his jacket and tie. However, I knew that this was as informal as he could bear to dress. "Would you please forgive me?" he asked the younger man, and then turned to me: "Sarah, could we go through to that little lounge at the back where it'll be quieter?"

I agreed and he immediately turned and started to walk away. Once I had paid for and picked up our drinks I followed him, but he had not been able to walk far; he was having to acknowledge other convention-goers who had recognised him as the creator of "Eleanor". It was probably a quarter of an hour later that we managed to find a couple of chairs together where we were able to speak with a little privacy.

"I've never felt comfortable at any literary events, let alone a science fiction convention," he said. "The first time I went to anything like this I was so excited to see some of my literary heroes that I wasn't able to talk to any of them."

"But now *you* are one of those heroes."

"Hardly. It was twenty years ago that *Eleanor* was published? My one and only novel."

"Why would you want, or need, to write another? It must have sold hundreds of thousands of copies worldwide?"

He shrugged: "But that's not necessarily been my doing, has it?"

"Whose would it have been, then?" I asked, and took a sip of my drink.

"Why, Eleanor's herself."

"Do you think of her as a real person?"

He laughed, and then shook his head, silent.

I prompted him: "When she was first conceived, when you thought her up, was she already fully formed and real?"

He considered:

"Yes, in a way, I think she was. It's just that at the start I didn't know her very well. I had to find out about her, and over time I thought that I had . . . When the book was published, and people asked me about it, it was as though she had gone from my life, and I was simply remembering an old friendship."

"You inscribed my first edition for me at the launch," I remembered.

"I hate to think how much you'd have to pay for it if you bought it today!"

"The first edition had quite a large print run, though, didn't it?"

"Something like two thousand copies. For a small press it was quite a lot of books, although nearly half of them were pulped after the first two years. The publishers were happy; even selling just a thousand or so made them a profit, and I got a reasonable royalty. We all thought that was the end of Eleanor in our lives."

"Was it a wrench for you when she left?"

"No. At the time I was glad we'd parted. You see, the novel had been going around in my head for years, and I'd written and re-written permutations on the same theme and the same character so many times . . . When the book came out and I was asked about it, I actually had problems remembering which of the various plots was the current one! But Eleanor herself was a constant."

"She came back into your life, though?"

"Yes. And that was why I was calling myself a silly old man."

"I'm sorry, I don't understand? I meant the Americans. What did you mean?"

He shook his head again.

"As I was coming down here, from my room, I shared a lift with Eleanor."

"What, your character?"

"Yes. She was standing there, in the lift."

"And did she recognise you?" I asked playfully.

He laughed again, but this time I saw tears in his eyes, and he had to turn away and wipe them.

"You see, I told you I was a silly old fool."

Once he had calmed himself David took a sip of his beer.

"You saw someone dressed up like Eleanor?" I asked. At length he was composed enough to answer:

"Yes, I suppose that's all it was. But for a moment it made me question everything. It made me wonder whether she was real or fiction . . . whether I had merely described a living person, or maybe I hadn't written about her at all. Maybe senility really is catching up with me?"

"You've still got *all* your marbles."

"Don't be so sure of that. I forget my keys, my spectacles . . . "

"Oh, I do that all the time!"

"But this Christmas I had a long talk with my granddaughter, Rachel, thinking her to be my daughter, Tanya. The poor girl was rather upset that her grandfather was starting to lose the plot. Don't worry, it's nothing horrible like Alzheimer's, but my doctor says, at my age, the onset of senility is no surprise."

"I'm sorry."

He shrugged. "When you get older it doesn't seem *quite* so terrible as it might have been when you were younger. I mean, it still makes me bloody angry. It's getting confused that upsets me most."

"And seeing someone dressed as Eleanor . . . ?"

"Exactly. I wanted to talk to her, you know. But she's not my Eleanor any more. As you say; 'the Americans'. She went away from me when we sold the rights to the book to that television company in the States. I never did see the pilot; perhaps, if I had, I would have vetoed the project."

"Didn't you even see the script before they made the series?"

"Yes, I did, but it was so different from my book that I actually felt guilty that they were paying me for it. I wouldn't have known it was based on my Eleanor if they hadn't told me."

"A few years ago I met the writer," I said. "He admitted that he'd read your book a dozen times and became obsessed by her. He fantasised about her living around the corner from him, and what the consequences would have been. That was why she was uprooted and placed in suburbia, kicking against the preconceptions of white, middle America."

"His Eleanor wasn't dangerous, like my Eleanor was."

"No. But it was quite radical at the time that she was even slightly alternative; a pierced nose and a tattoo, unable to cook and her house a mess . . . But she could still teach the perfect all-American little women around her the values of friendship, love, decency . . . It was heart-warming stuff."

"I never saw it, and I didn't want to."

"Did you see it when it was re-made though?"

"No. I was just happy to get paid twice!"

"The actress that the second company hired was much better. *Eleanor* became a hit over there primarily because of the actress—and clever marketing. They got it programmed prime-time on the biggest channels."

"Do you know," he chuckled, "we even banked a percentage of their merchandising? It included a whole line in women's fashion!" He smiled properly for the first time that evening. "No, I never met the American chap, but last year I finally met the Japanese artist who turned her into a comic book character."

"Did he apologise for ripping you off?"

"Yes, he was polite and very contrite. He claimed he didn't know at the time that he was in breach of copyright."

I snorted in an unladylike fashion: "But his graphic novels explicitly named your book as the inspiration for the series . . . "

And then I noticed that David's attention was elsewhere. In the doorway to the lounge was a woman with electric blue hair. She was obviously looking for someone. David half-rose out of his seat and seemed to be a little shaky on his legs. I got up to steady the old fellow and he looked knowingly into my eyes, and then immediately back at the woman. She was now walking into the main bar and out of sight.

"That was Eleanor," he said quietly. "Perhaps she was looking for me?"

"Perhaps. But then again, at these kinds of conventions there are always one or two women dressed up like her."

He looked at me steadily but excitedly, his eyes fixed on mine:

"No, Sarah. That was *my* Eleanor."

"The one you met in the lift earlier?"

"Yes, but also the Eleanor of my book."

"Shall I go and find her? I'll ask her to come over here and say hello . . . "

He looked nervous now, and agitated. I helped him to sit back down and he looked up at me:

"Would you do that?"

I went back into the bar but she was not there. Perhaps she had not found who she was looking for and was now searching elsewhere in the hotel? It could be that she had found whomever she sought and that they had left together. I went to the Welcome Desk in the lobby and explained to a couple of people from the convention committee that David Planer wanted to meet the young lady dressed like the heroine of his famous novel but they could not identify whom I meant. I described her as tall, with blue hair, dressed in the Goth style, but still they denied all knowledge of her.

On my way back to David I put my head around the door of the main conference room but it was empty. I looked into the bar once more, but she was not be seen there either.

"A part of the trouble," I explained to David an hour later in his room, "is that she doesn't look quite like the Eleanor from the television series, from the graphic novels, or the computer games."

"No, well, she wouldn't," he assented. "That's because she is the real Eleanor from my original book. And only I know what she looks like!"

The convention organisers had told him that as Guest of Honour, David could have whatever he liked from the mini-bar without concerning himself with the bill. We were therefore availing ourselves of the miniature bottles of spirits. He had decided that the so-called best bitter in the bar was unworthy of the name.

"Did you know that the Japanese fellow, I can't pronounce his name," David continued, "had his own model for Eleanor? I thought that comic artists would just make it up, out of their heads. But he drew a real person. Not that he told her! She was a woman he loved from afar, and he called her his muse!"

"So he had a habit of working without permission?" I asked.

"That's a little unfair," he chided me. "Once his comics really took off, and were published by a large corporation, they did the right thing and I received all my royalties."

He had calmed down by now. When I had reported back on my failure to find the woman he wanted to meet, he decided that he would like to return to his room. In my absence a very large, bearded Norwegian had been trying to explain something to David about the Velvet Underground and he looked relieved to be saved by me.

As we left the bar he had been rather unsteady on his feet, and I was a little worried about him. Now, sitting in his room swirling the drink around in his glass, he was relaxed and contemplative.

"But," he said, "I could see little relationship between the character I had created, and the gun-toting heroine of his comics."

"You have to call them 'graphic novels', especially at a convention like this. But I agree; as far as Japanese readers are concerned Eleanor is a weird-looking western woman rushing around beating the shit out of bad guys."

"And her sex life . . . "

"As a sub-plot it is bizarre."

"At least that doesn't get into the computer games!"

"Have you ever played them?"

He looked at me over the top of his spectacles with an expression that suggested that I did not know him as well as I thought.

"They're very good," I explained. "But they're based very much on the Japanese version of Eleanor."

"The strangest thing of all is to compare the American incarnation of Eleanor, all wholesome and good, with the Japanese one."

"But they do have a lot in common, apart from being skinny, with dyed hair, piercings and tattoos. All of them are outwardly strong characters but inside they're a mass of uncertainties and contradictions. I rather liked that description one academic gave of her as a 'flawed *femme fatale*'."

"My poor old Eleanor has been attacked by as many people as have defended her."

"The problem is, although she's a realistic, crazy, mixed-up woman, she's also rather sexy. No matter how multi-dimensional you want to argue she is . . . "

"Well, from her appearances in my book, through television and on to comics and now computer games, her character has been well explored . . . "

"Yes, but in all of those media she still *looks* like an escapist male fantasy . . . "

"Her fans include a substantial number of women; they say she's a strong, realistic role model."

"Post-feminist?"

"Exactly. But I suppose that at the end of it all, I'm jealous."

"In what way?"

"Well, if I'm to be quite honest, she was originally my own escapist fantasy."

"There's no sex in the book."

"Does there have to be sex?"

"No, I suppose not."

"You see, she was *my* Eleanor, and now she belongs to everybody."

That evening I took David down to the main convention room and stood by him on the small platform. I introduced him to the audience simply as the man who had created "Eleanor", and recommended to them that if they were true fans of his heroine then they really should read his original novel.

David then insisted on remaining standing, and even more than he would with me, he played up to the image of the elderly conservative who did not understand modern technology. He explained what books were, to those who had not read one before, and their advantages over other media with which, he admitted, he was not well-acquainted. He acknowledged the television as something he had seen in the houses of friends, and pretended not to understand anything about computer games or the internet.

He then talked about the *femme fatale* in literature, starting with Salome, and moving through to the heroine of Lawrence Durrell's *Alexandria Quartet*. This was as modern as he was willing to allow his literary references, but then he started talking of film and became more expansive. I knew that he had always loved the cinema and he obviously enjoyed talking about the alluring and seductive women of the silver screen who had so fatally used their charms to ensnare their lovers. Myrna Loy obviously had an important place in his heart, as did Theda Bara and the wonderfully named Musidora. He loved *film noir* and cited examples of *femmes fatales* played by Barbara Stanwyck and Rita Hayworth, and then moved on to the sixties and explained that along with Jules and Jim he too had fallen in love with Jeanne Moreau in François Truffaut's classic film. With a little embarrassment (at being almost up to date), he admitted to having been impressed by Sharon Stone in *Basic Instinct*.

He explained, though, that *femmes fatales* were not always the villains they seemed, and that the best are very often anti-heroines. Here he introduced the character of "Eleanor". He explained that he had set out to honestly describe a woman who had a strong sense of right and wrong, but, unlike most heroines, was really rather flawed. Because her many faults and weaknesses threatened to overcome her, she could only be viewed as an anti-heroine. He publicly apologised to her for endowing her with so many failings, but concluded by saying that there were enough of them to take the fancy of other creative minds, and hence she had flourished in the hands of other creative artists. They had explored sides of her personality that he had not even dreamed of.

I think that everyone went away from his talk charmed and amused, and hopefully some of them read David's novel as a consequence. At the end he agreed to answer a number of questions from the floor, but when he had finished, and I had to leave, he was still happily chatting to a number of fans who had further questions for him.

I went to the Welcome Desk, to find out what time our table was booked for dinner and, as I waited, the woman whom David had previously called "his" Eleanor walked past. I excused myself from the Desk and hurried over to her without thinking of what I would say:

"Excuse me," I introduced myself. "I was looking for you."

"Really? Why?"

"You came into the lounge this lunchtime, where I was sitting with David Planer."

"Oh?"

"Yes, and he commented that you are the double for his original 'Eleanor'."

"I'm sorry, but that doesn't mean anything to me."

"You know . . . Planer wrote the novel, *Eleanor*, that became the American tv series, and the Japanese graphic novels, and the games."

"You'd have to ask my husband. He's the science fiction fan. I'm just the long-suffering wife."

"Well, the character is pretty well-known," I replied, lamely. "*Eleanor* wasn't a science fiction book, but the science fiction crowd have rather taken her over."

She said nothing, obviously waiting for me to explain myself further.

"Planer is one of the guests of honour here this weekend, because the character he created is . . . ah . . . "

"So well-known?" she prompted.

"Exactly. And, well, the point is . . . other people have portrayed her, and depicted her, and none have ever been quite as Planer, the original author, ever imagined her."

"But *I* am as he imagined her?"

"Yes! And, well, this sounds a bit odd, but would you mind saying hello to him?"

"Of course not. I'm just going to find my husband, and then we'll meet you in the bar?"

I agreed and watched her walk away. I thought to myself that she didn't seem David's "type", but then realised that this was unfair of me. I had first met him when I was in my late teens and he was fifty-five, and he had always seemed to be a frail old man to me. There was no reason at all why he should not be attracted to a tall, strong woman in fishnets and leather-boots, with a shock of dyed blue hair.

I went to rescue Planer from his inquisitors and explained that he would be able to meet the woman he had seen in the lift. He asked "Does she know she's my Eleanor?" and I was able to say that I had explained the situation. He made hurried excuses to those who still had questions for him, and he took my arm and went eagerly into the bar.

We found "Eleanor" easily; it was quieter than before because a presentation had just started elsewhere. She was sitting with her husband near the door.

"I am delighted to see you again, my dear," Planer greeted her. The husband looked wary; he was a tall man with very long black hair, and his hands were tattooed in a Gothic script that I couldn't actually read. His body language suggested that he was very protective of his wife, but David charmed the both of them. For a half hour he talked as if the woman really were his Eleanor, and he explained, for the benefit of the husband, her various adventures and incarnations.

While he talked, I had the time to decide that David Planer's Eleanor was good-looking in an oddly individual way. Her features were slightly too large, but her freckles and her cheekbones were all that any of the artists that had depicted her could have asked for. Her figure was also real, unlike the graphic novel interpretation; she had very long legs, but I noted, with some satisfaction, that they were quite chunky, and although the make-up made her look younger, she had to already be in her early forties, and was therefore slightly older than I was. As with the Eleanor from David's book she had several piercings in her ears and one in her nose, along with a tattoo on her forearm. I have never thought piercings or tattoos to be particularly attractive and I was surprised that David, conservative as he was, did not condemn them on a woman.

"Would you like to know my real name?" she asked, towards the last.

"Oh no, please don't say anything!" he insisted in what may have been mock horror. "You *are* my Eleanor."

She agreed that she was, and that small incident summed up the meeting. She and her husband were both indulgent and considerate, and when they left they gave David their address in Montreal. They insisted that he should visit them, and he promised to try.

With old-fashioned courtesy he stood up as they did so, and as they left the bar he watched them go, beaming beatifically.

At length he said: "Thank you, Sarah."

"What for."

"For finding her for me."

The following day was the last of the convention and I was surprised not to see David at breakfast. I asked the hotel's front desk to check up on him and they assured me that he was fine but did not want to be disturbed. I didn't see him until after lunch when he came through to the bar to say goodbye. He looked tired and was walking slowly with all of his seventy years apparently on his shoulders. I told him so; I was worried, but he smiled indulgently and explained that the previous night had been the best of his life. He implied that something had happened after we had said goodnight, after dinner, but wouldn't say any more. He insisted, however, on us agreeing upon a date to meet one evening in a town where we would often rendezvous. Almost immediately his taxi arrived to take him to the station and back off to Lincolnshire.

℘

Although we talked briefly on the telephone once or twice, David and I were not in touch for another three weeks. When we met up for dinner it was where we usually arranged to meet. It was a small town with a choice of excellent public houses, and was conveniently mid-distance from where we both lived. We arrived separately, but at the same time, and walked from the car park together over the small bridge. I asked him if he was going to tell me what had occurred on that last night of the convention, but he said that I would need a drink in my hand first.

We had our usual choice of the three pubs that served food, and in winter we usually decided upon whichever could offer us a table near an open fire. This involved looking through the windows of each of them, and sometimes going in, only to leave again if the favoured spot was already taken. I was a little frustrated that he would not immediately tell me what had happened, but we decided on the Blue Bell without too much fuss. I sat at a table near the fire while he bought the drinks and came over with the menu. He then made it clear that he would not tell me his news until after we had made our decisions about food.

When all was settled and ordered, he leaned forward over the table:

"That evening, after you had formally introduced us, I saw Eleanor again."

"Ah, so that was what happened. I did wonder . . . "

"I went up to my room after dinner, and she was waiting for me. We talked for hours."

"What about?"

"About her, mainly. Oh it was lovely! And I don't think that she left until five o'clock in the morning. Fancy, an old fool like me entertaining a beautiful woman in my room until the early hours!"

"Lothario!"

"Well, there's more," he said, confidentially. "When she left I gave her my address. And just a couple of days afterwards she came to my place, for lunch."

"With her husband?"

"No, she came alone. You know that there are so many different Eleanors: the American Eleanor, and the Japanese one, and now the Canadian one . . . And you will want to know which one came to visit."

"Well, presumably, we're talking about the Canadian Eleanor?"

"No, we are talking about my original Eleanor."

"Not the woman from the convention? But she was the woman you gave your address to, surely?"

"My Eleanor and the Canadian one are so similar as to be almost indistinguishable. Even I can get confused between the two. I told you that senility is creeping in."

"What happened?"

"We had some business to discuss."

"What kind of business?"

"Well, it was to do with sorting out her life. You see, I left her slightly high and dry at the end of my book."

I did not have a comfortable feeling about this.

"We talked about all the things you'd expect," he continued. "The things you'd have predicted her to talk about; love, money, sex. We sat talking and talking and talking. She was next to me on my settee, and held my hand, and poured out her heart. She explained things that I didn't know from her past. And she told me what had happened after I left her at the end of the book. How she laughed at her American 'cousin', as she called her. And she admitted that she was afraid of her Japanese counterpart. And you know what really touched me, and made me happy?"

"No, what was that?" I asked warily.

"She said that, in many ways, she wished that she hadn't ever been taken from my book, and pawed at and ogled and looked up to, and despised by all those people who didn't even know her. But, I admitted to her that she had more than paid my bills for the last twenty years. It only seemed fair to be able to share it."

With a horrible clarity I knew what must have happened:

"You mean, you gave her some money?"

"It's her money really."

"Oh David! What have you done! She's only a woman who happens to look like your Eleanor. How much did you give her?"

"That's between me and her."

"She's swindled you! You silly old man."

"That's very uncharitable of you," he said, not at all annoyed by my outburst. "Eleanor and I discussed this at the hotel that night, so I was prepared. When she came to see me I had already been to the building society and it was all arranged. I gave her a cheque for four hundred and fifty thousand pounds."

"Oh David! Is it too late to stop the cheque?"

"Sarah, you are forgetting something?"

"What's that?"

"Eleanor is not real. I'm not that senile yet. Remember, I made her up, twenty years ago. She's only a character from a book."

"But *you* seem to be the one who's forgotten that! You're the one who gave her your life savings!"

"But what can a fictional character do with my cheque?"

"The woman who visited you isn't fictional, though. She's real enough, and able to cash that cheque."

He smiled at me and shook his head:

"No, Sarah. I tell you, it *was* my Eleanor who visited me. I knew what you would say when I told you, so I went to the Building Society this morning and confirmed what I already knew. She hasn't cashed my cheque. The money is still in my account."

℘

David told me that Eleanor visited him twice more during the following year. The first time she had arrived on an August morning with a picnic hamper and they had gone driving around Lincolnshire churches together. This would have been extremely thoughtful of her as it was one of his favourite pastimes, but it would hardly have been the way that any of the incarnations of Eleanor would have preferred to spend her day. Later, at Christmas, she had been with him for two days, staying overnight in his little cottage. She had never asked for any more money, apparently, and he told me that she had in fact bought him gifts. One was a rather bright red tie that he was very unsure of, but had worn to please her. Another was a very tasteful gold tie-pin, and as he had never owned a tie-pin before he rather treasured it.

She visited him again just before he died last year. He was seventy-two and went quietly in his sleep. There were a few obituaries, and two newspapers chose to print pictures of the television series Eleanor rather than the author. Radio Four read *Eleanor* as their Book at Bedtime, which they insisted was a repeat, but which I had never heard before. I think that there was only one sour note: an article in the *Guardian* complaining that Eleanor remained a very bad role model for women.

There was an impressive crowd at the crematorium and I helped his daughter, Tanya, with the arrangements. There were few family members, but many friends. All of these were outnumbered, however, by the admirers of his work, and by his work I mean the character he had created. The Japanese artist who had interpreted her in graphic novels flew over from where he was now living in America, but the writer of the television series who had first popularised her was not able to attend. Two different women had asked if it would be unseemly to attend dressed in their "Eleanor" costumes and David's daughter had begged them to dress as outrageously as possible.

I was asked to read a passage from the book of Job at the service, which I agreed to do, a little nervously. As I looked out over the mourners, those two women in their bright costumes stood out from the black that everyone else was wearing. I started to read the text that I had been given, and as I reached the part about an "iron pen" I looked up and saw for the first time the electric blue hair of David's Canadian Eleanor. I smiled at her, she grinned back, and I lost my place. Everyone was very understanding when I said that such a large crowd was a little off-putting, but how it would have pleased David. I returned to the beginning of the passage and managed to read it without making any mistakes.

After the service I stood with Tanya, her husband and their daughter Rachel as everyone filed slowly out past the flowers. The two women in their extravagant costumes were complimented by the family, and Tanya was very moved by the few words of obviously heartfelt tribute that the Japanese artist paid to her father. I could see the Canadian Eleanor coming towards us in the line, her dyed hair standing out from the typical shades of mourning. People seemed to move so slowly and it had been then that I calculated that at least two-thirds of them were really only attending because Eleanor meant something to them. And yet the woman that David imagined really was Eleanor was passing among them unnoticed.

When the woman came up to the family she said how sorry she was that David had passed away, and then recognised me as his friend from the convention.

"Hello," I said. "You live in Montreal, don't you?"

"That's right. My husband told me that Mr. Planer had died and I felt compelled to come over. It's my first trip outside of Canada since that convention. It'll sound silly, foolish even, but the old man had an affect on me."

"And you've really not been back to England since then?"

"No," she replied. "I often thought of it, to see Mr. Planer, but he might not have welcomed me."

"He would have loved you to visit," I assured her. "He was rather taken with you."

And then she was gone. I saw her in the distance later, but not to talk to again. At the time I wondered whether David would have left her anything in his will, but he had not. I was co-executor of his estate and I know that all the money went to his daughter and granddaughter. While finalising his financial affairs, I took the opportunity to look through his bank and building society statements, but no large sums of money had been taken from his account before he had died.

A few days after the funeral, once the will had been read, a very small party of us went back to his Lincolnshire cottage. It was strange to let ourselves in his front door without knocking, and to walk around his rooms, so fussily but tidily furnished. His two old cats had been re-homed, and a thin layer of dust had already accumulated on the polished surfaces.

Rachel was looking over a shelf of books in his study when she took down his own copy of *Eleanor*. She said that she had never read it, and asked her mother if she might have the book. Tanya took it and looked through it before handing it back to her, saying that her grandfather would have loved her to have it. I can still see her in my mind, sitting in the sun-lit small-paned window, reading those first few pages.

Rachel asked if I wanted to have anything of his to remember him by, but I could not immediately think what it should be. We went from room to room while she wondered what to keep, what to sell, and what to give away. Up in his bedroom she opened a wardrobe and despaired of what to do with so many old-fashioned clothes. It was on the back of the door that I saw his ties, and it was impossible not to notice a bright red one amongst them. Rachel thought this rather funny, saying that she couldn't imagine him ever wearing it, but I was able to tell her that he had done so, at least once, to please the person who had given it to him. I looked around the room for the little gold tie-pin and there it was on his rather prim dressing-table. Rachel was happy for me to take that as well as the tie, saying that he had been wearing it the day before he had died. David would call me a silly fool, but I keep them both on my bedroom windowsill with my signed first edition of his book.

Dispossessed

Everything went right for Jayne just as it appeared to be going wrong. Or, at least, that's what she assumed. To begin with she lost her home and her job. For ten years she had looked after the house of an old lady in Chelsea, and it was an enviable position. Jayne had just come out of college and a family friend recommended her to the elderly woman when the previous housekeeper left to get married. Jayne didn't think there could have been an easier job available, and for a decade all she had to do was make sure that the house was cared for. Her employer was looked after by nurses from an agency, and there was already a cook and a cleaner engaged. The old lady's dog, a large, rough-haired Scottish deerhound, ancient and lumbering, was looked after by the cook. For everything else, and there was very little else, Jayne had been at liberty to hire gardeners or handymen as and when they were required, and she simply spent a great deal of her time reading, watching the television, or entertaining friends in the large living room into which the old lady never came because she was bedridden.

Jayne did not take many liberties, but because the old lady was also deaf, her employer did not notice when Jayne's friends occasionally did. The wages were good, especially as Jayne was provided with board and lodging, and, in that way that one can be when young, it never occurred to her that anything had to change. But then the old lady died.

The family descended upon the house immediately, and to Jayne the old woman seemed to be buried with indecent haste. When the will was read immediately afterwards the house was divided up amongst a dozen different family members and they decided to put the building up for sale. Jayne was out of a job and had lost her home.

At the same time her relationship with Paul fell apart spectacularly. She was distraught that she only had a week to find somewhere else to live and her boyfriend, in front of all of their friends, made a callous joke at her expense. Jayne wasn't in the mood and she took it badly. He compounded her humiliation with another joke and then she said a few things about him which were quite unpardonable. There must have been a dozen of their friends present and their jaws dropped simultaneously. Jayne left the party immediately, and when she got back to the house she sat by the phone and waited to see who would call her. But nobody did.

She was too angry to do anything useful for days. The house was emptied around her; first by relatives taking the nicer items, and then by auctioneers who stripped the place down to the floorboards. Jayne swore at the family members and was ignored, and she even threatened the men from the auction house, who told her that they would phone the police if she didn't get out of their way. It all seemed to happen around her at great speed and she was powerless to do anything.

Jayne then made a mistake that very nearly got her into even deeper trouble. A van turned up outside the house and she let some tradesmen inside. She didn't care who they were or why they were there and she simply left them to their business, which was to steal a number of expensive light-fittings and other easily removed architectural features. Jayne hadn't realised what had happened until much later that evening when the estate agent arrived to look over the house and draft the particulars. The police were called, and the next day various family members had a meeting from which she was excluded, although they were obviously gathered to talk about the way in which she had let the thieves inside. One couple were convinced that Jayne had colluded with the men who, as far as they were concerned, had walked off with a part of their inheritance. There was talk of trying to press charges against her, although nothing came of this. However, the goodwill cheque that she had previously been promised failed to materialise.

On the last day she was in her bedroom, putting her few meagre possessions into black plastic bin bags, with no idea of where she was to go. A tap came at the door and a tall thin man introduced himself as Mr. Rogers. She had seen him about the house, with other members of the family, and had perhaps talked to him before. But she had not realised that he was aware of the position that she found herself in. Later, looking back, she supposed that she was still in shock, and she wished that her old friends might have made allowances for this at the time and perhaps offered to help her.

Mr. Rogers stood in the doorway and ascertained that Jayne now had no accommodation. He explained that he felt sorry for her and was annoyed by his own family for throwing her out on the street so callously. He was understanding, and after expressing what appeared to be genuine sympathy, he explained that he owned a large block of flats in south London and she was welcome to stay there, rent free, until she found something more suitable. She was not sure that she even thanked him, but she took the small manila envelope, which contained a couple of keys, and stuffed it into her handbag. He didn't say how long she would be able to stay there, but he said that the building was rather in need of modernisation and her neighbours would be mostly students. With a solicitous smile he suggested that he could arrange for someone to take her bags there, and so Jayne shrugged and simply left the dead lady's house carrying her handbag. As far as she was concerned the family were simply trying to get rid of her, and she complied. She was tired of fighting the inevitable.

Jayne walked out into the summer sunshine of the affluent Chelsea street in which she knew she no longer belonged. The old lady's ancient dog was the only creature to watch her go. She walked out and just kept walking, with no idea of where she was going or why.

It was then, at her very lowest ebb, that she met Andrew Hurst. He was sitting by himself outside a flower-bedecked pub and he asked her if she could tell him the time. She did so and he swore colourfully, surprising her. She didn't know why she had bothered to ask him what was wrong. After all, he could not have been in any worse a position than that in which she found herself. He explained, apologetically, that it was a long and stupid story and that she wouldn't want to hear it, but Jayne was in an argumentative mood. She insisted he tell her and he proceeded to relate how he had been taken in by a confidence trickster. A man who had claimed to be an old school friend had come up to him in the street and had somehow borrowed a hundred pounds from him. The deal had been that they would meet later, at that pub, when the man would return the money. Andrew admitted that he had known as soon as his so-called friend had walked away that he would never see him again, and he was angry with himself.

"It's just about impossible for me to sympathise," Jayne said flatly. "You see, I'm in a position that makes yours look trivial."

"Tell me?"

"And it's an even longer story."

"In that case I'll buy you a drink and then you can tell me."

And that is what happened. It seemed so natural to confide her troubles in a complete stranger, but he had asked for her story and so she told him, in exhaustive detail. She felt that by inflicting it upon him she would be somehow getting a small degree of revenge on somebody, but the result was something that neither of them could have expected. They went on to a restaurant and Jayne spent almost the whole night complaining. She ended up in his flat near the British Museum, and in his bed, and they were together for almost a year.

&

For weeks on end Jayne would forget that she had the keys to a flat in Balham that probably contained her possessions. Moving in with Andrew happened so quickly and so naturally that her previous life seemed to be something from the distant past, to be looked back at from across a great gulf of time. Andrew was very well-off; he had a position with a bank that sent him to various European cities and allowed him expenses that paid for her to travel with him. He bought her new clothes and jewellery, and had proposed marriage within a few days. These material things she accepted without complaint, but marriage seemed to be an altogether different proposition and she put him off time and again. Eventually he stopped asking.

Andrew told his mother that Jayne seemed to him to be something of a blank canvas. Five years younger than him, and considerably less worldly, he had introduced her to his twin passions of opera and rugby and in no time at all she had come to share his interests. Andrew's mother thought it an odd comment to make, but she soon saw his point, for her own interest in gardening was quickly communicated to Jayne and the young woman seemed happy to spend the weekends with her, helping in the garden at their house in Surrey.

Jayne's own family was small and distant, and Andrew's large and boisterous set of relations came as something of a revelation to her. They were immediately accepting of Jayne, and even took her part when Andrew bemoaned her lack of interest in marriage. She enjoyed their company, and life was good.

Andrew's announcement, a year later, that he was seeing another woman came like a physical blow to Jayne. He returned from work one evening, poured her a glass of wine and explained, awkwardly, that he thought that he might have found somebody else. She was unable to speak, unable to think; she looked around at his expensive apartment, full of his expensive things, and knew in an instant that she was no longer a part of it. She got up to leave, while he talked about helping to get her a flat of her own, paying her an allowance for a few months, and she decided that there was nothing around her that she could call really her own. He asked her to stay, to talk and sort things out, but she found her bag and her coat and simply left the building.

It had happened again.

It was a short walk to the main road where she would find a taxi, although she had no idea of where she would ask it to take her. Looking in her bag to see what money she had to pay a fare she saw in the bottom of it the crumpled manila envelope that she had been given all those months ago. The address was on the envelope, and she decided that she would go there.

The block of flats in Balham was not particularly salubrious. A four-storey red brick structure, it looked like it dated from the time of the underground stations, and was not in good repair. The door was covered with graffiti and had obviously been reinforced against vandals. The windows either side of it had been bricked up and the intercom had been smashed. She had two keys and the larger one effected entry.

In the dark hall a light came on automatically and revealed a staircase in front of her and short corridors stretching away to the left and right. The other key had a plastic cover over the top which bore the number twelve, and a small sign on the stairs showed that it would be on the floor above.

The door to her room, when she found it, was of featureless varnished wood, and once unlocked would not allow her inside until she had put all of her weight against it. Once admitted she ventured tentatively into a very small room, containing a bed, a small table and a wardrobe. The grey evening light came in warily through a frayed yellow curtain and Jayne's first thought was that it was a room for somebody to kill themselves in. It was in every way the opposite of what she had just left behind, or had been forced to leave behind, and the differences filled her with despondency.

The minute kitchenette and the bathroom with its small shower might have made her laugh if she had been able to draw on any inner resources, but all she could do was sit at the table with her head in her hands, unable to think about what she might do next. The rest of the world seemed a great distance away from that small, drab room, and she tried in vain to remember the name of the man who had given her the key to it. What had he done with the bin bags of her few possessions that he had promised to send along?

Eventually, unwillingly, she laid down on the bed, very still. There were other tenants in the building and she heard them coming and going during the evening and late into the night, making more or less noise. She listened to the sounds of the building, amazed that just as it seemed to be quiet at last, another door would crash shut somewhere above or below, or she would hear footsteps, or a distant cough. Somebody had a dog, somewhere, and from time to time it would bark, monotonously, for minutes on end.

It is always disconcerting to wake up in a strange room. Jayne found it doubly hard to work out where she was because she could not remember quite where she had expected to awake. The large, modern, airy bedroom she had shared with Andrew was already something from the past, and was certainly a place now denied to her. Remembering the circumstances in which she had been given the keys to the cramped flat brought back memories of the room in the old lady's house. But she didn't seem to be able to recall where she had ever lived before that time.

Hunger sent Jayne out to buy breakfast in a small café, and then she walked around the district to get her bearings, spending time in an arcade of stalls selling antiques, but buying nothing. As she looked at the jewellery and ornaments, silver and brass, glassware and pottery, they all looked like so many items that had once belonged to people who were now dead.

The miserable mood stayed with her as she returned to the flat. She had not brought any provisions back with her to prepare her next meal, or even a cup of tea, and she was standing in the middle of the main room, indecisive, wondering what to do, when there came a knock at the door.

She remained still and said nothing. She continued in silence after the next knock, but then a key was fitted into the lock and the door started to open.

"Hello? Who is it?" she demanded, frightened, backing away.

"Oh, you're here? It's Terrence Rogers," stuttered her visitor. He put his head around the door nervously. "Only, I've knocked from time to time, and never found you in before." He opened the door and stood half in and half out of the room. "I was worried, because you never seemed to be here. I didn't know whether to let the flat to somebody else. If you don't want it, that is."

Jayne said nothing; he took this for acquiescence and somehow insinuated himself inside the room, with the door half closed behind him. They faced each other over the small piece of thin carpet, both in their coats.

"You look well," he suggested awkwardly, to which she gave a short, noiseless laugh. "Are things not okay?" he enquired solicitously.

"No, not really," she admitted.

"Can I help at all?"

"Being able to come here helps, I suppose," she said, wondering how it could possibly be that she was grateful for such an unpleasant place to live. In every respect the flat was dingy and depressing and all that she wanted to do at that moment was leave. If this man (she had forgotten his name again) had not been standing between her and the door she might have rushed out immediately, and perhaps returned, ignominiously, to Andrew.

"You're very welcome to stay here as long as you like," he smiled, revealing a set of small teeth that were yellow and a little too far apart from each other. "I just didn't know if you were using the flat."

"I wasn't, but I might be. I mean, well, I've nowhere to stay again."

"I'm sorry to hear that. Do you have a job at the moment?"

"No, I didn't need one. I was with someone . . . " she started to explain, and then decided that she would rather not tell him anything. "But I'll have to get one."

"Well, don't concern yourself about the rent until you've got some money coming in. And then we'll sort something out. You know? We'll come to an arrangement. And I can always offer you something better than this."

"Oh, don't worry," she shivered involuntarily. "I'm sure I can find something else on my own."

"I do have other properties, nicer properties, that you could stay in."

"I'm not sure what work I'll be doing. I mean, I don't know what I'll be able to afford, or where would be convenient."

"Don't worry," he tried to sound reassuring. "As I said, we can come to some arrangement."

And then Jayne seemed to be watching the claustrophobic scene being played out, somehow, from outside of herself, as if she was watching it through a camera placed high up where the wall met the ceiling. What happened didn't seem to be happening to her directly.

The man took a tentative step towards her with his hand out, and when she didn't react he took another step and put the hand on her forearm. Jayne was unable to move, for she did not seem to be the same woman as she was watching down in the room. She looked on, and listened as he reassured her of his friendship, and his desire to help her. Because she did not move he seemed to gain in courage and took her other arm. He gave her a kiss on the cheek before letting her go with a smile that suggested he had made a conquest. He was relaxed now, and brought out a packet of cigarettes from his coat pocket. He asked if she minded him smoking and Jayne shook her head.

"I have a nice flat coming free at the end of the month," he considered. "Near Victoria, very central, but it's up high and you can hardly hear the sound of the traffic."

Again she said nothing, being rather more interested in the displaced view of herself and the room, and wondering if this was what was meant to be an "out of the body" experience. Surely it was only meant to happen to people at the point of death? She felt curiously indifferent to everything, even the thought of dying, but then she did not feel that she was going to die.

The man had his cigarette in one hand and a lighter in the other, but he did not put the two together. He was too busy talking about the flat she could stay in, and then he took another step forward.

"I really like you," he said, quite grave all of a sudden. "And I'd like to make sure that you're okay, and looked after."

An alarm was sounding somewhere in the distance, as though the woman below was trying to communicate somehow with the woman above.

"Is there anyone looking out for you at the moment?" he asked. "Anyone who cares for you?"

Jayne was wondering if the woman below would answer, and when she didn't he put his cigarette and lighter back into his pockets. He took a further step forward and kissed her softly, tentatively on the mouth. Suddenly his hands were inside her coat and she could feel them over her, around her, and with a shriek she pushed him away.

Jayne had returned to herself. She hadn't seemed to feel anything at the time, but now she could remember how his stubbly face had pressed itself against hers, and the way that one hand had clutched at her waist while the other pressed at her breast.

He was apologising, mumbling now after all of his eloquence.

"Please leave," she said simply, wiping her lips clean of his spittle, and pulling her coat closed. She felt as though her clothes were all rucked-up, rearranged and uncomfortable.

"Don't be like that," he said, apologetically, looking at the ground. "I like you a lot. I thought you might like me. I mean, I've helped you, and there's more that I can do."

"I don't need your help," she said quietly, fearful for the first time, feeling exposed and vulnerable.

"But you do," he said slowly, looking at her now with more confidence. "You've had my flat for free for nearly a year. And you're welcome to keep using it. You do rather owe me . . . " he started to say, and then became defensive again. "I don't mean in any monetary way. There's no proper obligation, nothing written down. What I've done for you I've done out of friendship, and I supposed you might like to be friendly in return, that's all."

Jayne was now firmly back in her own body, although the emotion she felt was something quite alien to her. There was an anger inside her that she was not repressing, but channelling. With deliberation she asked.

"How do you want me to repay you?"

"Friendliness, just friendliness," he said, half pleading, almost grovelling.

"In what way would you like me to be friendly?"

"However seems right to you, and natural."

She considered, and nodded, letting her coat fall back open.

The man smiled and walked forward very cautiously. With a careful, slow movement, as though he did not wish to startle her, he put his hand forward and onto her waist.

"Is that all right?" he asked.

Jayne said nothing, but tensed up at his touch. He moved around to her side and put his face into her hair. She heard him breathe in appreciatively, and then she felt the hand move down and it was going inside her skirt.

"No," she said, and reached down and stopped him. He started to resist her attempt to take his hand out and she forced the nail of her thumb into his wrist.

He shouted out, but she did not release her grasp. He tried pulling away, and suddenly she was able to direct all of the pent-up fury and aggression through her whole body, down her arm, and into her thumb. She felt her nail break the skin, and still she pushed while he shrieked and shrieked. Still she pushed, not seeing anything around her but concentrating her energy into forcing her thumb into the wound while the man thrashed and flailed. She felt her nail break and still she pressed until he managed to hit her, somehow, and she fell over onto the floor.

She lay looking up at him; there was blood all over the man. He was hugging his arm to his chest and looking up at the ceiling, not wanting to see what she had done to him. "Why did you do that? Why did you do that?" he was repeating wildly, taking his breath in deep, sucking lungfulls.

Jayne sat up cautiously, scared of the man who himself seemed very frightened. Her chin hurt where he had hit her, but her neck was more painful; his punch had knocked her head back with a jerk.

He was obviously in a worse position than she was. His white shirt was black with blood, and it had run down and was staining his trousers.

"I thought you liked me?" he said, now sounding hoarse, still looking fixedly at the ceiling.

She was worried that he would turn on her, so she stood up carefully, slowly, ready to run to the door. She was thinking of how quickly she could get there and open it when a voice from outside called:

"You all right in there? I thought I heard screams?"

The man now stared at her, fearful, and she called back:

"All right now, yes. We had a fight, there was an accident. But we're okay."

"Are you sure?" the voice asked warily. "I was worried."

Jayne went cautiously to the door and opened it far enough to look out at a young man, with an even younger woman standing a couple of paces behind him.

"Thanks for checking," she said, with a composure she did not feel. "I was being very stupid, but we're both okay."

"Good," replied the young man, nervous and unsure, but obviously relieved that he could back away and leave. Jayne saw him go to the stairs, and then, keeping the door open in case she needed to escape, she looked back into the room. The man still stood there, stiffly, holding his injured wrist up to his chest, and the blood was now starting to puddle around his feet. She shut the door cautiously but kept her hand on the lock.

"I think I've cut one of your arteries," she said slowly.

"Shit," he said through his teeth. "It hurts so much I want to cry. Do I need an ambulance?"

"Probably."

"I'm sorry; I think I can feel something running down my legs."

"It's blood."

He laughed; he was trying to keep down the hysteria: "Is that good? I thought I might have pissed myself."

"That might have been better.'"

"I have to keep pressure on it, don't I?"

She shrugged.

"What shall I do?"

When she didn't answer he looked down, apprehensively, to where he held his hand, and then, fearfully, took his wrist from his chest. It adhered slightly to the sodden shirtfront, and he stared down at the wound she couldn't see. His eyes rolled upwards as his head fell to one side and then he collapsed in a noisy and ungainly heap on the floor. His bleeding wrist was flung out, wound uppermost, and Jayne watched while the blood pulsed outwards.

She had still not closed the door, and drawing her coat around her she left the room, the building the street and the unconscious man whose name she could still not remember.

Jayne took a taxi back to Andrew's flat; she had no idea of where else to go. She still had a key and let herself inside cautiously, but he was out at work and she had the place to herself. Her coat had hidden her bloodstained shirt and skirt, and she immediately stripped off in the bathroom, threw these in a bath of cold water, and took a shower. Details of what had happened came back to her, but she made a conscious effort to try and repress them.

When she turned off the shower she listened, but the police were not yet knocking at the door. She dried herself quickly and in the bedroom found that Andrew had not taken her clothes from the drawers and so she was able to get dressed. Back in the bathroom she tried to get the blood out of her clothes. It came out of the lining of her coat surprisingly easily, but her blouse was stained and so was her skirt; in desperation she doused them in cleaning fluid.

Looking in the mirror she could see that she had a bruise on her chin which was now hurting more than her neck, and she could say that the man had hit her first. She had been trying not to think about what had happened, but she decided that if asked she would say that he had tried to assault her; she could argue that she had grabbed his wrist in self-defence and what had then happened was the result of him refusing to take his hand out of her skirt. She repeated this to herself time and time again, rehearsed her explanation, making herself believe that her version of events was true. There were questions that might be asked, though, such as did she let him get too close when she could have sent him away? Had she really needed to keep driving her nail deeper and deeper into his flesh? She tried not to dwell on them, though they kept coming to the surface of her mind. She had the most trouble not questioning why, even now, she had not called an ambulance for him?

The cleaning fluid had removed the stains from her blouse and this now simply needed rinsing several times to get rid of the smell, but her skirt was ruined and she threw it in the bin outside. When all was straight in the bathroom she had to wash her hair again so that she would be able to dry it and get it straight, and then she applied her make-up.

By the time Andrew returned from work she was almost calm. However, when she saw him she lost all of her self-possession. The scene that followed was emotional and confusing, because at first he assumed her mood was entirely due to his revelation about the other woman. Time and time again he assured her that he had made a mistake and he wanted her, Jayne, after all, but she did not seem to listen or understand. He was entirely in the wrong, he insisted, and he pleaded with her to forgive him and to come back. Finally he began to understand that there was more to her distraught state than his own actions.

Eventually she was able to recount her story; the story that she had rehearsed so many times over the previous few hours. Andrew's reaction was that she should simply call the police and report the assault, at which point she had to admit that she had left the man, probably bleeding to death. How, she demanded of Andrew, as if it was his fault, was she to explain the fact that she had not called an ambulance.

He poured them both a drink and took time to consider what they should do next. Jayne was relieved that he should want to take over the decision-making, but then took some convincing when he decided that he should go back and check on the man. He calmly explained that her reaction to the assault was quite normal in the circumstances, although it would certainly complicate matters. He suggested that they return to the flat and review the situation when they had ascertained how the man was. Perhaps, he suggested, whatever they discovered, all they had to do was remove her possessions from the flat, and nobody need ever connect her with what had happened there. It was with the greatest reluctance that she got into his car later that afternoon and returned with him to Balham.

They were able to park outside the door. The building did not look any different to her, but he pointed out that there was a large sign, only partly vandalised, advising no entry. The downstairs windows were all boarded up and she admitted that she had not noticed any of this before. After his insistence that they go back to the flat he now seemed reluctant to go inside and even insisted that the key would not work. She now took it from him and, pushing at it violently, opened the door.

Inside she pointed up the stairs, and as they started to ascend they heard footsteps in the corridor downstairs.

"Hoy!" called out a voice and Jayne's heart, already low in her chest, sank, and she could not stop herself from leaning against the wall, then sliding down it to the floor. They waited until a man came in sight, and she was surprised that rather than wearing a police uniform he was wearing a fluorescent jacket and a hard hat.

"You're not supposed to be in here," he insisted. "How did you get in?"

Andrew held out the key.

"Is she all right?" the man asked, nodding towards Jayne sitting on the floor.

"She's fine, just a little tired," Andrew said. "We just wanted to visit one of the flats."

"They're all empty. There's nobody here. The place is due for demolition next month."

"We'll only be a couple of minutes."

"I can't let you do that, sir."

"It's not dangerous, is it?"

"No, sir, not exactly, yet. But next week they'll be coming in to strip out what can be salvaged; then it will be."

"In that case," Andrew explained coolly, "Won't you look the other way for a few minutes while we visit the flat of an old friend, for old times' sake?"

"Well, if you make sure you're gone in five minutes . . . and you understand that we didn't see each other . . . " he conceded. "But only five minutes, mind."

"We won't be any longer," Andrew agreed. "And we didn't see anybody."

As the man walked away Andrew helped Jayne to stand.

"He didn't say the place was being demolished," she said weakly.

"Who? The man who attacked you?"

"Yes, him."

"Well, maybe you were too upset to realise what was going on?"

"Perhaps," she agreed, and led him reluctantly to the door to the flat, just off to the left at the top of the stairs. Andrew tried the key, but the lock refused to move. Jayne leant back against the wall of the corridor and waited while he fought to get the door open. When he had succeeded she refused to go in with him. She watched him walk inside and try the light switch, which did not work. Through the partly opened door she heard him move across the room and open the curtains and then there was silence, a brooding silence that seemed to echo up and down the corridors just as surely as any shout would have done.

Then she heard movement again, but could not decide what he was doing inside. Eventually he reappeared at the door, frowning:

"He's not in here."

"Is that good or bad?" she asked and, taking a deep breath, walked forward.

"But there is something," he started to say, hoping to stop her going inside.

He was too late. Once in the doorway she could see the black shape on the floor by the wardrobe and her heart lurched so violently that she thought she would be sick if her throat had not suddenly constricted, and then she saw that the large form lying there was not the man. There appeared to be a large, dead dog lying on top of a small pile of black plastic bin bags. Something hammered in her temples and she felt dizzy. She could not be sure, but it looked like her former employer's dog.

Andrew went over and knelt down by the dead animal.

"Is this your stuff?" he asked, pulling out some books and cassette tapes from the bag nearest to him.

She nodded.

"Well, then let's take them and get out of here."

He tried to pull the bags out from underneath the body of the dog but they ripped and the contents spilled out. Gathering together a number of items he tried to add them to the one bag that he had managed to retrieve.

"Shit," he said, looking at his hands. "All this stuff's covered in blood."

"Leave it," she said quietly.

"But these are your things."

She backed out of the room.

"Leave it all."

"No, wait a minute," he was calling to her as she turned and started to run to the stair. "I think this animal might still be alive."

"Leave it!" she screamed. "Leave it!"

Bloody Baudelaire

For Rosalie

I.

Lucian Miller always cherished his memory of the short time he spent at Cliffe House. Almost immediately afterwards he became so frightened of forgetting details of what had happened that he wrote it down. He returned to his account time and again over the years; nostalgia was a vice with a grip on him that he refused to relinquish.

Above all it was Miranda Honeyman he wanted to remember. He needed to permanently fix her in his mind as she had appeared to him on the night of the arguments, on the night when it had all gone so horribly wrong. He didn't want to lose the image of her as always elegant, and wearing one of her habitual tight dresses that fitted close, all the way down her slim arms to her wrists. He needed to be able to see her wonderful red hair in his memory.

Of course, describing the Miranda of Cliffe House meant describing Gerald Kent, her partner, and Lucian did this with reluctance. Gerald was tall, with black hair and round glasses that were affected, Lucian was certain, as a pose. Lucian disliked him from the start, before any jealousy played a part.

"The green shadows in the moist evenings of summer . . . " Gerald had intoned.

"Fucking shut up!" Miranda replied, apparently uninterested.

Lucian, Elizabeth and Adrian were all looking over to where the couple stood under the tall elm tree, posing in the shadows, forming an artistic tableau.

"I don't know whether to be amused or frightened by them," Elizabeth whispered in Lucian's ear.

Adrian, his school friend, overheard her: "Neither, only embarrassed."

As Miranda was Adrian's sister, her brother's discomfort was reasonable, and the fact that Elizabeth could not understand them did not surprise Lucian. But he was impressed by both of them.

"The green shadows in the moist evenings of summer," Gerald repeated theatrically.

Miranda saw the three of them staring and walked slowly over to where they sat out on the terrace:

"Baudelaire, he's always quoting bloody Baudelaire."

Lucian felt she was right to suggest that Gerald was becoming a bore.

Elizabeth nudged him. When he turned to her she frowned as if to ask just where had he persuaded her to come for the weekend?

At the same time, across the table Adrian looked down at his shoes and mumbled, almost inaudibly:

"You really shouldn't have stayed."

"You invited us," Lucian replied quietly.

Miranda now stood there, one hand on her hip, and drew deeply on her thin cigarette. Lucian marvelled that it was hard to tell it apart from her long white fingers. Was her red hair dyed or natural? Either way it made her face look pale. She was five years older than him and he believed her to have a sophistication towards which he could never hope to aspire.

"Did the moist green shadows remind you of that quote?" Lucian was bold enough to call across the garden to Gerald. "Or did the quote create them?"

"Lucian!" Adrian complained.

"The *green* shadows in the *moist* evenings of summer," Gerald corrected him and, aware that he was too far away to properly command his audience, he followed the red-headed woman over to the terrace.

"I'm sorry," Lucian apologised.

"Gerald isn't," Miranda pronounced. "It gave him a chance to say it again. He's too tedious."

"Oh, you do embarrass me with your compliments," he replied as he walked over. Once he reached them he drew close to her, trying to kiss her neck. She turned and slapped him, the sound echoing sharply off the red brick walls of the house. He pretended to stagger backwards, as if dealt a mortal blow.

"Well, I don't recall you ever attempting to compliment *me*," she said. "You're far too self obsessed."

Metal abruptly grated on stone as Adrian pushed his chair back and stood up. He glared at Miranda for several seconds, his brows screwed up contemptuously as if he was about to start shouting at her. Instead he turned and stormed into the house.

"It's the height of bad manners," she called after him, "to leave your guests to entertain themselves." Her words trailed away as it became obvious that her attempt at humour had failed.

"Well," Gerald shrugged, "I'm glad Lucian and Elizabeth are only guests. I'd hate to think of them as permanent fixtures—rutting away like that in the spare bedroom."

Lucian was mortified by the comment, but even more horrified at what Elizabeth's reaction would be. He didn't dare look at her, but he had heard her immediate intake of breath. He decided that he should act unconcerned and said, rather precisely:

"I apologise if we made too much noise last night."

Elizabeth now stood up. He turned and saw that her appalled expression was directed at him rather than Gerald. She too fled inside.

"You bastard," Miranda turned to Gerald with disgust. He, however, simply shrugged and walked back out on to the dark lawn, lighting another cigarette.

Lucian didn't know what he should do. He thought that there ought to be a way to retrieve the situation but the alcohol that they had been consuming all day slowed his thoughts.

"Ignore him," Miranda insisted, leaning over the table conspiratorially and stubbing out her cigarette in the ashtray.

"Perhaps we should leave?" Lucian proposed.

"Why? Surely Elizabeth appreciates that Gerald was *trying* to upset her? She shouldn't let him succeed."

"Adrian obviously regrets that he invited us."

"Forget him. He's always like that. He's got nothing to complain about. I'm the one who should complain about him."

"Why? What's he done wrong?"

"Oh, nothing. It's just that he's always here, getting in the way."

"I understand. I've got two sisters . . . "

"No, you don't understand. He's not even my real brother."

"Oh."

"He's my step-brother, marooned here by my step-father when he left, after my mother died."

It was obviously a subject that annoyed her. She sat down opposite him on the edge of a reclining chair.

"I'm sorry," he said, deciding to try to disentangle the family relationships later.

"What? Sorry that I've been lumbered with a step-brother I don't want?"

"No," he floundered, "for your parents dying." There was an uncomfortable silence. He felt a fool. He could not believe what he had said.

"Really, don't worry about Adrian's little tantrum," she forced a wide smile. "He'll get over it. All we need to do is reassure Elizabeth that Gerald isn't worth worrying about, and then we'll get on with the weekend."

"I hope she isn't upstairs packing her bags."

"She seems a bit highly-strung?"

"Yes, perhaps—well, no," he shook his head. Persuading Elizabeth to come to Cliffe House had not been easy, but until that moment the weekend had been everything he had hoped for.

"What's the problem between you two?"

"There's no problem."

"Of course there is. I'm not stupid."

"I'm off to University next weekend; Exeter. I'm going to study Engineering."

"And you're leaving her behind?"

"No, not quite. She's going to University as well, but to the other end of the country; Leeds."

"Oh," she said simply as she filled her wineglass from the remains of two opened bottles on the table. She then lay back in the chair, kicking off her shoes. She closed her eyes and Lucian watched her face as it relaxed. Her cheekbones had been the first feature that he had noticed when he had met Miranda; they were strong but softly moulded. Her lips, too, were slightly exaggerated, large and rather bitten-looking. He tried to imagine how they would be if she wore lipstick. Her eyes were lost in the shadow of a rather eccentric burgundy hat that had now tipped forward.

"Are you going to try and keep your relationship going long-distance?" Miranda asked.

"We're going to try, but she's convinced it won't work."

"What do you think?"

"I want to give it a try. But I'm scared she might be right."

The orange streetlamps flickered through the trees from the town below: a breeze had risen ominously as though the summer's fine weather was preparing to break. It was late, and only now did it seem a little too cool in the shadows that seemed to creep out from under the eaves and the close-pressed trees. A chill had poured out from the dark vegetation at the edge of the lawn and over the dark, mossy grass. As if liberated by the night, the ivy seemed to encroach over the terrace and the walls of Cliffe House. The building had not been properly maintained for years and he could almost hear its soft, crumbling decay. The overgrown garden seemed to want to reclaim the hillside.

Gerald flicked his cigarette into the black shadows and walked back over to them.

"I ought to go and see if Elizabeth's all right," Lucian said to Miranda quickly, hoping to make his escape.

"Of course she is," Gerald had heard him and waved Lucian to sit back down in the chair. The younger guest hesitated and his host came up to the table. Lucian assumed that he had something else to say, but Gerald offered nothing and simply attempted to fill his glass from the nearest bottle. Only a small amount of wine dribbled out and he put it down in disgust.

"Well," Lucian considered, and then said with resolution, "It's time to retire anyway."

He mentally flinched, expecting another attack, but Gerald looked serious, concerned even:

"Ah, sleep, every evening's sinister adventure," he mused. "It may be observed that men go gaily to their beds with an audacity which would be beyond comprehension did we not know that it is the result of their ignorance of danger."

"More Baudelaire?" Lucian asked.

"Yes."

"It sounded more like H.P. Lovecraft," Miranda said, opening her eyes, but there was no smile this time. She leant forward and took a cigarette from the packet.

"It would to you," considered Gerald, following her example. In later years Lucian would realise how pretentious they both were, how affected, but at the time he was taken in.

"I'll go on up to Elizabeth," he said decisively.

"Ignorance of danger!" Gerald repeated, laughing, and Lucian wished that he had the inspiration to say something clever in return.

Lucian and Elizabeth had arrived the evening before, ostensibly as guests of Adrian. They had been treated to a long, civilised meal during which they all discussed Gerald Kent's paintings. Lucian had liked the man's arguments, but when they were later shown some of his work he was not convinced that his fine theories had been translated onto the canvas. The trouble seemed to be that the pictures were too cold and lifeless.

Finally, some time after midnight, they were able to go up to bed. Lucian and Elizabeth had been given a large room, with white walls and a blue rug on stripped pine boards; a double bed was the only piece of furniture. Like the rest of the house, the room was dusty and badly in need of repair and redecoration, but they did not notice this until the next morning. The room was still hot from the scorching day, and opening the window had failed to relieve the heat.

It was the first time that either of them had made love, and they were able to take their time without fear of disturbance. And waking in the cool of the clear Saturday morning with Elizabeth—naked, smiling by his side—Lucian knew that it would always be a precious memory.

But now, when he entered the room that following evening, it was dark. The curtains were drawn against the night and they moved in the breeze from the open window. He could hear the first few drops of rain being blown against the glass.

"Go away," Elizabeth said sulkily from the bed.

He walked over slowly and put his hand out in her direction, touching her shoulder. She was still dressed. He tried to stroke her hair but she pushed him away, telling him to leave.

"Elizabeth," he started to explain, faltering, not knowing what he should say, but trying to assume the right tone.

"Go away," she said with more resolve, and he stood up, with a sinking feeling in his stomach. He recognised the determination with which she had argued so many times before.

He walked slowly to the door and waited there, annoyed with Gerald for having precipitated this mood. Just how annoyed was Elizabeth, though, at his reaction to Gerald's stupid comment? He was finally reassured:

"Give me a while," she said quietly. "Let me get ready on my own."

His despair of a moment before was gone and he rejoiced that all was not lost. Excited, he imagined how it would be to come back to the room when she had composed herself. Of course, the atmosphere at breakfast on Sunday morning might be awkward, but there was still the night to pass first.

He shut the door softly behind him and decided that he would give her twenty minutes.

℘

Down in the living room an old standard lamp was glowing in one corner, throwing odd shadows around a room that was draped with scarlet material and cluttered with heavy furniture. It looked much better by artificial light than it did during the day. The effect that they sought was Eastern, with material gathered up to the centre of the ceiling like a sheik's tent. The colours looked rich, deepened by the shadows, although by daylight it had all looked rather faded, stained and old. Miranda walked in a moment after Lucian and asked after Elizabeth.

"She's all right," he reported casually. "I'll go back up to her in a while."

Miranda sat down heavily in an overstuffed armchair by the window. She took a book from the floor beside her. Immediately afterwards Gerald Kent attempted to make a more dramatic entrance:

"Well, what great entertainments have we planned for this evening?" he bellowed in a stage voice. "I'm pleased to see that you're not going to bed yet."

"Shortly," Lucian insisted.

"Of course," he agreed. "But not before we have consumed vast quantities of alcohol."

"No. We've been drinking all day," he replied.

"We've really hardly started," replied the man as he went to a low table with bottles and glasses on it. He proceeded to pour out three large whiskies. "I propose a game of cards?"

"I don't know," Lucian said, but he wanted to placate the man. "Five minutes," he offered. "Then I'm going up."

Gerald passed a glass to Miranda, who took it without thanks, and he put another down in front of Lucian. Then he proceeded to hunt through a sideboard, presumably for cards. After some cursing he eventually found a battered packet and placed it on the table. He pulled out a chair, turned it around and sat on it backwards.

"What are we playing for?" he asked.

"I didn't realise that we were playing for anything?" Lucian replied, deciding to take a sip of the whisky but immediately regretting it.

"Of course you are," replied Miranda, not looking up. "But I warn you, all Gerald can play is poker. He doesn't do anything unless he can make money at it. His motives are always mercenary."

The man laughed heartily, but unconvincingly.

"What about his 'art'?" Lucian asked.

"His reason for painting me is that it turns him on," she replied. "You see, it also turns other people on, and they pay him large amounts of money for the pornography that I've posed for."

"But if that's the case, *why* do you pose for him?"

"Because it turns her on as well," the artist replied.

"It's quite a convenient arrangement, really," she admitted.

Gerald leant back in his chair and picked up a pad of paper from the table. He ripped off a piece and looked around the room.

"Don't you have a pen in this house?" he asked Miranda, but she ignored him. He got up again, angrily, and started to look through the sideboard once more.

"Deal the cards," he ordered.

"Treat him nicely!" Miranda insisted

"I can treat him how I like," Gerald said. "He comes here, eats our food, drinks our wine, enjoys our company. We give him a bed so that he can screw his little girlfriend."

"If you want us to leave," Lucian offered once again, not quite confident in front of Miranda, although annoyed enough now not to want to take any more abuse from Gerald.

"He's like your so-called brother, Miranda, another parasite. And he's like you in many respects. For aren't all the lovers of great men but parasites?"

Miranda looked up and frowned. Lucian pretended to peer at his cards and like Gerald, who had found a pen and was trying to get it to work, he watched as she got up out of her chair. She stretched and took measured steps to the drinks table where she put down the book and placed her cigarette between her lips. She picked up a half-full bottle of port. Still frowning she looked at Gerald and then down at the bottle that she now weighed in her hand. When she looked up again she and the artist smiled at each other.

Miranda brought the bottle up to her shoulder and threw it at Gerald with all her strength. She was slow, though, giving him plenty of time to react. All he needed to do was lean back against the sideboard. It flew from her hand, hit the sideboard, and was deflected against the curtains where it then fell and broke in a less than dramatic fashion on the floor. There was a sound of breaking glass a second later as a pane in the French windows beyond the curtain fell out.

"Shall we leave?" Lucian asked Miranda, almost desperately.

"Stop offering to leave!" she rounded on him, talking with the cigarette in the corner of her mouth and looking levelly into his eyes. He looked down at his cards and tried to concentrate on the fact that he had a king and an ace of the same suit.

As though nothing had happened Gerald complained that the pen refused to work.

"Use matchsticks." Miranda pointed to the fireplace as though the scene between them had never happened.

Gerald took the box and threw it on the table. "Say that each represents five pounds?"

"I don't have that sort of money to play with," Lucian was horrified.

"What's the point? A pound then?"

"Okay," Lucian conceded, knowing what cards he had at that moment. "But only a couple of hands, and then I'm going upstairs."

Gerald Kent resumed his chair and lit a cigarette from his own packet. As he exhaled, the smoke wafted in Lucian's direction and made his eyes sting. Miranda also took a cigarette from the remains of her own mutilated packet.

The painter stared suspiciously at his cards:

"Do you want another?" he asked Lucian.

Lucian said no and Gerald dealt himself a court card. Immediately he threw his hand down in disgust. Lucian showed him his cards and Gerald simply flicked a matchstick across the table.

The host dealt once more and lost the hand again. For a while they seemed to win alternate hands although Lucian remained slightly ahead. It was about ten minutes into the game that Gerald decided to raise the stakes to five pounds. Lucian wanted an excuse to go up to Elizabeth and so agreed to two more hands only, calculating that he could lose them both and come out owing nothing.

They started to bet with several matchsticks at a time, and twenty minutes later Lucian was able to triumphantly declare:

"There, I've cleared him out."

He piled his matches neatly and put the cards on the table between them. He stood to leave and looked expectantly at the artist.

"Cleared me out of what? Two hundred and fifty pounds at most," Gerald dismissed his success. "It's almost worth losing if such a small amount makes you happy."

"Of course, what's important is a well-fought battle," Lucian suggested smugly. He was about to add a caveat about the usefulness of two hundred and fifty pounds, but Gerald cut in:

"Well, if it's not the money, then you won't mind playing again."

"I'm sorry. I'd like to go to bed now."

Miranda looked up from her book:

"You can't do that. You've got to give him a chance to win his money back."

"It's not the money," Lucian agreed unwillingly.

"In that case we'll double the stakes," his opponent declared. "No, let's say two hundred and fifty pounds a time. That'll make life easier."

"That's too much," Lucian replied; he did not want to give up what he had won.

"You can't leave the table without giving him a chance to win his money back," Miranda repeated herself, apparently uninterested.

"You mean letting him win it all back in a single hand?"

Lucian might even have accused Gerald of cheating if Miranda hadn't seemed to be colluding with him.

There was no reply from either of them. "All right," he surrendered, reluctantly picking up the cards, shuffling and dealing them. "But I can't afford to lose anything at these stakes."

"Good, but before that, another drink?" the artist asked.

"No thank you," Lucian replied, firmly this time. "I haven't touched the earlier one. I told you, I'd like to wake up in the morning with a clear head."

Gerald Kent lost, and continued to lose. They silently played more hands than Lucian had intended. To the accompaniment of the house creaking and settling into the cooling night he won hand after hand. Eventually Gerald had one matchstick left and Lucian recommended they give up. The artist still said nothing and dealt the cards once more. He picked up a third card for himself, which was low, and then another of the same number. Then he picked up one more that was too high.

"Bastard!" Gerald exclaimed grimly through the remains of the cigarette between his lips.

"Are you still losing?" asked Miranda from the other side of the room.

"I don't believe in earning money in a conventional manner," he replied. "So why should I lose it conventionally?"

"It's a pathetic way of losing money," Miranda told him.

"No, you've got it all wrong, Miranda, my little philistine. It is the noblest way of losing money. Losing as much as I have takes great skill!"

"Yes," Lucian agreed. "And he has skill in abundance at the moment!" He warily calculated how much money

Gerald owed him and reckoned it in the thousands. "I've taken all of his money off him again."

"Good," said Miranda. "He had far too much anyway. I'm ready for bed."

"So am I," replied the artist, as if indifferent to all that had happened.

"How much are you down?" Miranda asked.

"Not much. Double or quits on a hand?" he asked Lucian as though unconcerned at the reply.

They both stared at their guest and he knew that they would deem a refusal as impolite.

The hand was played slowly. The artist tapped his foot all through the game, giving away his nervousness.

Lucian was dealt two cards identical to his very first hand, a king and an ace. It beat Gerald's eight and ten.

"Sorry about that," he apologised.

"No you're not," Gerald replied.

"Yes he is," noticed Miranda. "And he shouldn't be."

"The same again?" asked Gerald.

"No." Miranda was annoyed. "Lucian's luck will have to run out at some point. And he's won that money fairly."

"It might last a little longer," Lucian said weakly.

"Double or quits once again," declared the man. "But first I need another drink."

He arose and walked over to the drinks table. He took up a bottle of brandy and, joking, threatened Miranda with it. He then poured out a liberal measure and walked over to where she sat by the fire.

He snatched up the book and tried to read it.

"Give that back, you bastard."

He raised an eyebrow:

"Not until you stop swearing."

"Arsehole."

"Well, you're definitely not going to get it back now."

"Give it to me," she insisted, still sitting. He flicked through the pages:

"*The Book of Jade*," he announced.

"Give it here," she jumped up from her chair and snatched the book back from him. "You started that game of cards so you bloody well finish it."

"Okay, okay," he put his hands up to defend himself in mock fear. Then he turned back to Lucian: "Well then, double or quits."

Again the game was played in silence. This time Gerald needed anything other than a court card to win. He turned over a king.

"Bastard! Again!"

"I'm going to bed," said Miranda.

Gerald considered: "Let's say all the money that you've won off me tonight against all the money that I have and will have when my next exhibition is over?"

The next hand was started. Miranda circled around behind both of them.

"You have a morbid desire to win," she told her partner. The artist did not take up the challenge: he was engrossed in his cards.

Lucian was desperate to lose now and leave. When he was able to he said: "You've beaten me." He put his cards face down on the rest of the deck and picked it up to shuffle it. He was annoyed; the whole game had been a charade.

"No you haven't!" Miranda declared, tired. "I saw your cards. You cheated, you lost that game on purpose."

Gerald stood up, his face black with anger:

"You made yourself lose that hand. I've never been so insulted. You patronising little shit."

"No, I mean I'm sorry," replied Lucian, angry himself. "But I can't take all of your money," he added lamely.

Gerald Kent sat down, slowly.

"We'll play that one again."

Lucian won once more. He could not believe that his luck had lasted so long. The odds against it were preposterous. "Let's play again," he insisted, needing to lose.

"This time it's all that money against all of my canvasses."

"They're not all yours to give away, are they?" pointed out Miranda.

"All of the canvases in the house . . . they're of Miranda, but she doesn't own them."

Miranda drew herself up and looked as though she were about to attack him.

"Do you always paint Miranda?" Lucian asked, trying to diffuse the argument that was threatening to distract them.

"I am the only inspiration for his art," she said slowly, barely containing her anger. "It annoys him, though, because he hates not being given complete credit for his work."

"That's not true," the artist protested.

"Of course it is! You're floating around with your head in self-generated clouds of hot air until someone says, 'well, if it wasn't for Miranda, would you be as good a painter?' "

"Well, if it makes you happy, dear," he insisted.

"Why don't you try painting anyone else?" Lucian asked. "Or something other than nudes?"

"He has, but as I said, I'm the only inspiration for his work. Anything else that he tries to paint just comes out worthless."

Gerald nodded, but as though he hadn't really been listening. He wanted to get back to the game, as did Lucian whose hands were sweating. The room felt airless.

He believed that surely he had to lose and they would be where they had been at the start. He dealt the cards, unnerved, however, that his opponent was looking even more concerned than he was. The artist would not have normally allowed Miranda to put him down like that.

The hand was played slowly. Lucian had a poor set of cards and decided that despite his previous failure he would simply try to play badly. Miranda had not seen his hand this time and could not accuse him of cheating. Unfortunately his opponent's cards were even worse than his and still Lucian won.

"My talent then," the artist proposed.

"This is stupid," Miranda moved around behind Lucian.

This time, Lucian decided, he would play as well as he could, hoping that a change in tactics would stretch his luck beyond breaking. He knew the whole game was pointless. They were just going to continue until he lost a hand and they were quits once more. He simply wanted it to happen as soon as possible.

However, he won again. The other man said nothing.

"Well," Lucian was embarrassed. "That's everything then."

"No, there's me," pointed out Miranda.

"You're not my possession," Gerald replied

"That was a nice thing to say," she smiled at him. "I don't think that you believe it for a second, but it was a nice thing to say."

"I wouldn't want to own you if you were giving yourself away," her partner smiled.

"The feeling is mutual, my love. So come on, play for me."

"Yes, all right, we'll play for Miranda then," Lucian agreed.

"This *is* stupid," the artist finally conceded.

"That's what we've both been saying," Lucian insisted. "So just take back what I've won off you."

"No way."

"Then we'll keep playing double or quits 'til I lose."

They proceeded slowly. After a few moments staring at his cards Lucian's opponent put them face down on the table and walked over to the drinks. He picked up a bottle:

"Wine can clothe the most sordid hovel in miraculous luxury, and conjure up . . . "

"Finish this game," shouted Miranda. He poured himself out another whisky and continued as he walked back over to the table:

"And conjure up many a fabulous portico in its red vapour's gold, like a setting sun in a clouded sky."

"Bloody Baudelaire," Miranda informed Lucian.

"None of these things, my dear, equals the poison that flows from your eyes, from your green eyes." Gerald picked up the card that he had been dealt. How he reacted; he slammed it back down on the table and stormed out of the room into the hall. The door crashed shut behind him.

"He can have it all back," Lucian told Miranda. "I don't want it. We've all had too much to drink and . . . "

"Rubbish! We haven't had nearly enough. And no, you won everything fairly. It's all rightfully yours."

"He must have it back." Lucian was talking to himself.

"No, you've got it all now. Don't get too excited that you've won his talent, though. That's worth very little."

He was deeply uncomfortable as she stood over him:

"I don't want what I won off him tonight," Lucian protested, more upset than Miranda seemed to realise, but she ignored his feelings:

"What plans have you got for me then?" she taunted him.

He said nothing, feeling completely out of his depth.

"Oh, just fuck off!" she shouted at him and turned and strode over to the door. As she left she slammed it shut just as the artist had done. Lucian did not move.

Almost immediately there came raised voices from the stairs. He wondered how long he and Gerald had been playing cards and whether Elizabeth was still awake. He knew he should have gone up to her ages ago, but how could he have left the card game without causing another scene? He wanted to go up immediately but didn't want to face Miranda or Gerald. A minute later they were shouting outside the living-room door and Lucian was afraid that they would come in. He stood up, expectant, but then he heard the front door open. There was a shout and then the door was opened and banged shut again.

And then it was quiet. Lucian waited a few more minutes before daring to creep out and up the stairs. The door to his room opened only a little, but it was sufficient to see that Elizabeth had put the back of a chair under the handle. He called to her but she refused to reply. It was very late and he knew that he had stayed downstairs for far too long. He also knew that he would not be able to persuade her to let him in.

He returned to the living room where tiredness and the drink caused his head to swim and he had to sit down. Looking up at the ceiling he could see where the strange arrangement of material was sagging under the weight of fallen plaster. There was also a massive spider's web that he had seen earlier that day, but which now had a vast spider sitting in it, surveying its domain.

It had all gone so badly wrong. The wind had risen and was rushing through the trees outside. The rain was now being dashed hard against the windows. Lucian felt miserable and closed his eyes, hoping it would stop the dull throbbing at the front of his head.

৪০

When he opened his eyes again he knew that he had slept, but perhaps not for long. He felt very cold. The front door was open and an icy rush of wind found its way through into the living room.

"Miranda? Gerald?" he called out. In response the lights were abruptly thrown on and the woman swung around the door frame, tossing her coat on to the settee.

"Ah," she greeted Lucian as they both squinted at each other in the artificial brightness. "Not in bed yet?"

"Well, no. I'd fallen asleep. Where've you been?"

"Out," she replied simply, looking around and finding a packet of cigarettes. "Making sure he doesn't come back."

"Oh?"

"I've thrown him out."

"Really?"

She looked as though she were in pain. She was very wet and her hair looked black, plastered to her head. When she lit the cigarette he noticed that her hands were shaking badly. She inhaled gratefully.

"Best thing I did, of course. I don't know why I ever took up with the bastard."

"So why did you?"

"It's a question I've asked myself countless times." She drew in the smoke once more and then let it out, kicking off her muddy shoes. "Inertia, probably. Gerald was older than me, and when I first met him he seemed exciting and fun and clever and all those things I later found he wasn't." She sat down on the edge of the sofa, shaking with cold, and Lucian could see the water soaking into the material where she sat, and dripping off her onto the carpet.

"You should see him sketch out a figure on canvas and you'll see that he can be inspired . . . Gerald was once full of wonderful ideas. Now he's successful and embittered. We've grown apart, though we've been together so long we've grown together."

"I don't understand."

She had to wipe the water from her face where it ran down from her bedraggled hair into her eyes. "Love is many things," she said, tired and apparently bored. "It's never had much to do with sex. I suppose the highest form of love was when we walked together. When we were chatting, or even lost in our own thoughts. Then we would merge into one person. We've walked into each other until we're half way inside of one another. It's like we were superimposed."

He frowned: "I still don't understand. And you're using the past tense."

"I know I am. I told you, I've thrown him out. I've got rid of him. He's dead to me."

"What did you mean, 'superimposed'?"

"That once upon a time flesh merged, but it wasn't sex. We got so used to each other that we did everything without even bothering to communicate. We walked to the left, out of the door, and up the stairs. We went into a shop, bought things, but not once did we talk, discuss what to do next . . . "

"I don't think I'd put it so morbidly as you."

"No? Then how would you put it?" she asked sarcastically.

"Well, you just get to know a person after a while. Is familiarity such a bad thing?"

"No," Miranda admitted, shaking her head. "That would be all right. That I could put up with."

She got up and walked to the table with the bottles of drink and poured herself a small measure of whisky. The back of her dress was muddy, and she had left a dark wet stain on the settee. Lucian declined her offer of a glass and recommended that she really ought to go and get herself dry. She nodded and downed her drink in one mouthful. Instantly she grimaced and grasped her stomach. Steadying herself against the table she retched. When he moved over to help her she waved him away, then looked around for the packet of cigarettes once more. He wondered what had happened to the last one.

"No, I know what you mean, but we weren't like that," Miranda leant uncomfortably against the wall. "We walked together, his arm around me and slowly my arm pushed its way into him. His flesh opened up."

Lucian looked doubtful and Miranda smiled wryly, drawing in the smoke of the newly-lit cigarette, then blowing it out very slowly.

"There was no raw flesh, no blood and guts. I just slowly disappeared inside him. You see, we didn't just do things together. What we did were things that he wanted to do. I didn't argue."

Lucian agreed that it didn't sound like love.

"Perhaps I shouldn't complain," she considered. "It was the one time when I was wonderfully nothing. I did not exist. I was merely a part of him, doing what he wanted to do. I hate myself for it now, but at the time it was like being asleep, perhaps like being dead. But it wasn't the same when we actually made love. That was something different. Though there were times during sex when I wanted to sink my teeth into his shoulder, to burrow my head into him."

"You've drunk too much."

"You can be so boring sometimes," she declared with unexpected hate. "Isn't there anything interesting about you? Last night you went upstairs and your little Elizabeth gave herself to you. And I suppose it was all so lovely, and now you know all about love and sex?"

"That sounds like jealousy."

"Of course it's jealousy! But there's more to life than . . ." Miranda stopped.

"Yes?" he asked. "Go on."

"Yes, I'll go on, because it's not a contradiction to say that easy and happy existence isn't what we should strive after." She thought; "Experiences . . ."

"Now you really are talking rubbish," Lucian laughed, surprising himself as much as her. "And you're contradicting yourself. You said that you felt great when you were unaware of anything, when you didn't exist."

"It's a vice like cocaine: I love it, but I feel so bad about it."

Suddenly she retched again and put one hand to her mouth, dropping the cigarette as the other hand clutched at her stomach. She ran out and Lucian picked up the cigarette and put it in the ashtray before following her into the kitchen. When he got there she was spitting vomit into the stainless steel sink.

"Can I get you anything?" he asked, but again she waved him away. He stood, useless, in the middle of the room. She was properly sick now, her body convulsing and the liquid splashing around the sink. When she had finished she seemed to relax a little, then turned on the taps to wash away the mess and then cleanse her hands. Calmer now, she poured herself a glass of water. She sipped at it and then spat it out, staring after it into the sink. Lucian stood quietly, waiting, and watched as she then took a bottle of cleaning fluid from the cupboard and poured it liberally around the sink before rinsing it away. Again she washed her hands and only then did she turn and look at him. She reacted as though she had not known he was there.

"Give a woman a bit of privacy," she demanded, and then ripped off some kitchen roll and wiped her face.

He backed out into the hall apologetically and walked, unthinking, up to the front door. He tried to look out of the glass panes but all that he could see was his darkened reflection, and the distorted mirror-image of the hall.

Without turning he was able to see her leave the kitchen and walk away to the conservatory. Although he didn't think he should follow her, he was not convinced that they had finished their conversation. He certainly didn't want her to have had the last word.

He found her in Gerald's studio, standing before the canvas he had been working on. She was standing absolutely still and looked pale:

"I'm sorry. I shouldn't have said all of those things," she said.

Lucian decided that he would not appear to forgive her immediately.

Other canvases lay around, though only this one was well lit. The painting was a study of a nude woman half lying on her back with her hair out behind her on the floor. Life-size, there was something magnificent about the model for all that the painting was not finished. The skin was milk-white but with a hesitant suggestion of colour. The red hair was a little too bright, a little too unreal.

It would have been hard for Lucian to recognise the model if he had not known that she was standing beside him. As Gerald so often did, he had painted her so that her face was turned away.

"It's going to be an amazing painting," Lucian said.

"Well, it's yours now."

"What do you mean?"

"You won everything at cards."

"He's going to look pretty silly when I have to give it all back to him."

"He won't be coming back," she mused. "Remember, it's all yours."

"Where's he gone at this time of night?"

"Who knows? He's probably half way to London by now, or France," she laughed. "And quoting Baudelaire to himself . . ."

Lucian and Elizabeth had not been shown that particular work-in-progress on the previous evening, but like those they had seen he found it hard to explain what it was about it that he disliked. He could not understand why Gerald painted with such cold colours. Beyond the canvas, on the far wall, was a large mirror and he could see Miranda in it. He compared the colour of her skin with Gerald's grey representation of it.

"You're wrong to call it pornography," he said, but Miranda did not reply. "It's not designed to titillate."

By making her turn her head away Gerald was denying her any personality, he decided. Perhaps by being dismissive of his subject he was being dismissive of her, but that did not seem to Lucian to be the point. He obviously had a genius for painting a woman's body; in the picture before them he had posed his model in an awkward attitude and he was giving himself a greater challenge in capturing her image successfully. He had painted her from the side, and from only slightly above, and he had accentuated the thinness of her arms at the expense of the torso. For no apparent reason he had made her breasts very small. Somehow it was all distorted, although only slightly so. It was slightly cruel, or mean.

Next to the easel, on the floor, were several smaller canvases. Lucian knelt down and gingerly removed the cloth that covered them. These were the pictures they had been shown the night before, and he ranged them about the easel. They were a third the size of the new portrait, but all were of Miranda in various poses. Each had a different coloured background, shadowed so as to imply a curtain, but obviously not representational. He had to admire the way that brush strokes, apparently so effortless, could hint at such a subtle variety of skin tones and shapes. But while it seemed such a waste that they were so grey and lifeless, they were nonetheless fascinating. He stared at them for some time, considering whether the fascination came from the paintings or the subject herself.

"You don't like them?" she asked.

He realised that he had been looking at them proprietorially and put them back and re-covered them with the cloth.

"No, you don't," she decided.

"They're very good, but they don't seem quite, I don't know . . . They don't capture their subject." No, they were not quite Miranda, they were not quite correct.

"Are these what Gerald had talked about for the new exhibition?" he asked.

"His very early work would probably be more your style," Miranda suggested. "More Russell Flint."

Lucian didn't understand the reference.

"Do you have any of those here?" he asked.

"There's one upstairs."

She stood there for a few moments and then told him to follow her. They went through the house, turning off the lights behind them, going up to her bedroom. The low wattage bulb inside revealed a mess; clothes hung over the wardrobe door, over the chair, over the end of the bed. They were suspended from the curtain-rail by wire hangers and must darken the room by day. And there were more clothes piled on the floor in shapeless heaps. The dressing table was cluttered with make-up and bottles, and the bookcase overflowed with paperbacks and magazines. There were boxes and bags, often filled with further boxes and bags, and there was no surface that was not covered, whether it was with ornaments, curios or costume jewellery.

And it was a dusty room, though not dirty. The bed had various blankets thrown over it and was unmade.

On the wall in a corner was a tiny painting of a nude. Lucian did not immediately recognise it as Miranda. She was much younger, very pretty and quite plump.

"It's lovely," he said as he moved closer to it.

"I was quite young then. Nobody's features are properly formed at that age."

"It's not like the ones downstairs," he admitted, squinting at it.

As he stared at it Lucian sensed movement behind him and glanced round. Miranda was removing her wet dress so he turned back to the picture, having seen nothing untoward, and determined that he shouldn't. He could hear her open a wardrobe, close it, and then walk out of the room. He could tell that she had gone into the bathroom, and he studied the painting closer. He stared at her breasts in the picture, with their big pink nipples, and he felt aroused.

When she returned he started to pick his way through the debris on the floor to get to the door. She sat down on the bed, in an oversized shirt tightly buttoned at the wrists, but from which her long legs stretched. "I suppose that picture's yours as well."

"I ought to let you go to bed," he said, refusing to reply to her comment.

"Don't worry about me. I feel quite awake now. I'm happy to talk. You can go to bed if you want to."

"Well, no, perhaps not immediately."

Lucian did not want to admit that the door to his room was barred. Miranda's bedside clock suggested that it was just after three o'clock.

After a pause she said:

"I really need to clear all the junk out of my life, and Gerald is a good way to start." She looked amongst the old papers on the bedside table and produced one last cigarette from a packet that she then threw towards the door. Then she hunted for something to light it with.

"I'm going to have a great big bonfire with all of Gerald's stuff."

"Won't he be annoyed?"

"He won't be back."

"Why not just box it all up and throw it in a shed?"

"There's too much. In fact, it'll take me weeks to burn all his stuff. You've never come across such a hoarder."

"I don't know . . . my mother . . . "

"No, I promise you, you've never come across anyone like him. He's so full of his own self-importance. He kept everything. And anything that wasn't of immediate use was boxed up and labelled and filed. And why? Because he expected it to be of interest to other people some day? He kept a diary since he was eight because he thought future scholars would want to pore over his every word, reading them to divine his motivation long after he had gone. But it's rubbish; he only had a mediocre talent. When he moved in here he brought all his shit with him."

She finally found a small green disposable lighter down the side of the bed. When her cigarette was lit she drew in a very appreciative lungful of smoke and patted the blanket beside her for Lucian to sit down.

"I suppose we all keep too much stuff . . . " he tried to explain.

"You really don't understand. It wasn't unreasonable that he might want to keep his old sketchbooks and canvases, but his old clothes? His old shoes? Magazines, and other rubbish? You wouldn't believe how much utter shit we accumulate in our lifetime. Most people throw stuff away eventually, but not Gerald. And he made collections of all kinds of things throughout his life that made it worse."

"Like what?"

"Like birds' eggs, butterflies, stamps, matchbox tops, cigarette packets, but never long enough to put together anything of value."

She dropped the cigarette into an old cup by the bed and then lay back and looked up at the ceiling: "The day he moved in here I expected him to bring a suitcase, but he brought a whole bloody removal lorry. And it's all going to be burnt."

Miranda stopped and put her hands over her face. Lucian wondered if she was tired, or had a headache, but then realised she was sobbing.

"Hey," he put a hand on her arm. "It's okay."

He manoeuvred himself to her side and she put her head on his chest and one arm over him, seeking reassurance. She wiped her eyes, annoyed, but stayed in the position in which they found themselves.

"I'm so stupid, ignore me," she said.

"No, you're not," he tried to reassure her. She was silent once more and he stared down at her red hair. He stroked it and she did not object. He played with a lock of it that fell about her ear. There were little blue flowers embroidered on the shirt that was wide open around her neck. When she had moved he could see and marvel at her skin, taut over her collar-bone. He could not begin to understand why Gerald, when he painted her, would not give it the deep, warm tones that he, Lucian, could see, and which appeared to him to be so beautiful.

There was an ugly red mark under her eye, though, and a cut on the side of her face by her ear which was bleeding.

He didn't think that Miranda had noticed that he was staring at her, but she moved once more, rolling over and looking away from him. Lucian was almost overwhelmed by tiredness and without thinking he lay down by her.

"Gerald wrote his diaries for posterity." She was almost inaudible, perhaps talking to herself. "He wrote them for people to read after he'd gone. And that included me. He knew I'd read them . . . he left them lying around. And he was very cruel."

She rolled back over to face Lucian.

"I don't know you, but you seem like a decent person."

He was flattered.

"I always used to fantasise about this house," he admitted. "I passed it every morning on the bus to school. I couldn't see it during the summer, of course. It was only when the leaves were falling from the trees in autumn that it appeared. And in the winter evenings, of course, it was too dark. There was rarely a light burning at a quarter to five when the school bus passed."

"What did you imagine it to be like?"

"Inside, all decay and grandeur. Lofty rooms, dark red shadows and dust."

"You weren't far off. But you knew my step-brother lived here with me?"

"No, we were never in the same class—not until this last year."

"Does the house live up to your expectations?"

"It exceeds them."

She put her arm over him to squeeze his hand and he squeezed it back. He was thinking about what she said, thinking of how to reply, when he saw that she was asleep. The house still creaked as they lay there, finally settling for the night. Lucian lay next to her, their noses almost touching. She seemed young now, like a little girl, her mouth half open, her eyes closed. He was considering getting up, turning off the light and finding himself somewhere else to sleep, but he was so tired and so comfortable that he did not want to move just at that moment. His eyelids were heavy and itchy, and although he was enjoying looking at Miranda he must have closed them for a moment and almost immediately fell asleep.

II.

Lucian awoke on Sunday morning with a great presentiment of doom. Starlings seemed to be squabbling under the eaves and rain was being dashed against the window in uneven bursts by the wind. He could tell it was late and his head hurt abominably. He was alone in Miranda's very dishevelled bed, and was still dressed from the night before. He was too hot with the sheets pulled up over him.

He got up immediately and looked out between the curtains and the clothes that hung on the rail. He could almost see the wind coming at the house across the miles, gaining speed and force until it met it on the hillside, the first object in its path. It came up the valley from the English Channel, following the tidal river that gave the town below its name. The wind brought the rain horizontally so that it was penetrating the walls, forcing its way between joints and frames. It came in around the edges of the loose panes of glass, and dribbled out quietly beneath the windowsill. He closed the curtain against the too-bright light.

Once out on the landing Lucian could smell bacon cooking. He looked warily through the open door of the room that he was meant to have shared with Elizabeth, but both she and her bag had gone. Before going downstairs he had to visit the bathroom and was glad to find headache pills and health salts. He locked the door and felt safe for a moment from whomever might be left in the house. It was only a temporary refuge and he wondered just who he would have to face downstairs; who he would have to apologise to for the night before. He told himself that nothing was entirely his fault, that he was the victim of events as much as anyone else, but he was unsure how far he could reasonably argue this. Not feeling any better, and not daring to look in the mirror, he walked back onto the landing.

His room really was completely devoid of Elizabeth's presence. She might possibly be downstairs, waiting to leave, but it was unlikely. There was a chance that she would have simply got up and left, and would not have tried looking for him, but it seemed doubtful. As long as she had not looked in Miranda's room. As long as she had not seen him sharing Miranda's bed. If she had, he hoped that she would have at least noticed that he had been fully dressed.

Lucian descended the stairs uncertainly, and from the hall glimpsed the debris in the living room from the night before. He could hear someone moving about in the kitchen, but who it might be, and whether they were alone he could not tell. He assumed it would be Miranda, but would Adrian be up as well? The hall clock said that it was half past one.

He took a deep breath and walked into the kitchen. He tried a cheery "Good morning" as he entered the room.

Only Miranda was there. She was wearing a large white dressing gown.

"A bacon sandwich?" she asked, not turning around.

"No, thanks."

"You should, it'll make you feel better."

He decided that she might be right and so agreed. She passed him a sandwich on a plate, presumably her own, and went back to making another.

"Things haven't exactly turned out well," she told him, "after last night."

"Somehow I guessed they wouldn't have." He sat down at the table gloomily.

"Adrian left a note to say that he was so embarrassed by me and Gerald that he's going up to London to stay with his father. Well, that's fine by me, though as his guest you have every right to be pretty well pissed-off with him. And it means that his father will phone me up later and give me all kinds of grief based on Adrian's stories. That's not a problem either; I'm used to it. The little bastard emptied my purse before he went; for his train fare, I assume. And Gerald has left as well, or, rather, I threw him out last night. I'm sure he won't be returning," she stopped making the sandwich and appeared to be looking out of the window. "That's good, I know it is."

"Are you sure?" Lucian asked.

"Yes. Intellectually and emotionally, I'm sure. But I've relied on the bastard for the last ten years and it feels pretty strange. It leaves all kinds of complications."

"And Elizabeth?"

"I was saving that news until last."

She finished making her sandwich but she didn't turn around.

"When she shut the front door behind her this morning I woke up. I caught up with her half way down the drive so you probably wouldn't have heard the poor girl expressing her opinions."

"She wasn't happy?"

Miranda finally turned round and faced him.

"No. She woke up on her own. When she came out to look for you we'd left my bedroom door open. She saw the two of us."

"But we fell asleep fully dressed?" He used the anticipated excuse.

"Yes, but I half-woke up at six this morning because it was so cold; the weather's changed you know. I was surprised to see you there, but I decided just to pull the covers up over us both. I've put the heating on since then, and . . ."

"You did tell her that it wasn't how it might've looked?"

"Of course I did, but she wasn't in the mood to listen."

"I was meant to go up to her," he explained. "But we started playing cards, and I wasn't allowed to finish the game until I'd won everything."

She didn't reply, but sat down at the table opposite Lucian. He noticed that she had a bruise forming under her eye, and the cut on the side of her face had a new scab on it but was starting to bleed again.

"Perhaps it's for the best?" she suggested hopefully.

"You may be happy to see the back of Gerald, but I'm not so happy to lose Elizabeth." He took a bite out of his sandwich and his stomach lurched.

"Do you love her?"

"Of course."

"No, really, do you love her? Is it really the end of the world that she thinks you've been unfaithful?"

"It's pathetic, isn't it? But I think so, yes."

"She said," and Miranda smiled at this, "that if you try and contact her she'll tell your parents about everything that's happened this weekend."

"Ouch."

"I suggest you give her a few days to calm down. If you're meant to be together as a couple then you'll get over this. And don't worry, she isn't going to tell your parents anything."

"I really don't know what to do."

"Of course you don't, but you're welcome to stay here for as long as you like. Lie low. No matter how bad things seem right now, they'll be a little bit easier by tonight, and tomorrow it'll be even better still."

"I'll still have to face Elizabeth, and try and explain."

"And how pathetic do you sound? If she really loves you she'll come and ask for your side of the story. Let her prove her love. But ignore me. I'm sounding like a bloody agony aunt. But what's a couple of days staying here? It can't get any worse. Inaction is no great crime."

"Thanks."

He looked over at her and noticed that there was blood coming through the material of her dressing gown at the arms. It was no surprise she had thrown Gerald Kent out if this is what he had done to her. Lucian thought about asking Miranda about her cuts and bruises but could not summon the courage.

After breakfast the clock chimed the half hour as he passed it in the hall. He felt better for having talked to Miranda, and though he doubted her advice, it was easiest not to question her reasoning. Miranda was older, a woman of the world, he told himself; she knew what she was talking about.

Lucian shaved and showered and found his last change of clean clothes. He decided he would telephone his parents later to tell them that he was staying for a few more days. They wouldn't mind him being away, but what he would do with his time there he didn't quite know.

Washed and dressed, his head felt clearer and he made his way back down the stairs and sat for a while in the living room which still bore the evidence of the previous night's battle. He was reading Miranda's book when she appeared in the doorway. She had changed out of her dressing gown and was wearing a sheer grey dress. Once again he wondered at the woman before him and the woman of Gerald's pictures. The dress was tight under her breasts and tailored around her stomach. As with all her clothes the sleeves were tight and reached down past her wrists, accentuating the length of her arms. She had her red hair tied severely back, and the dress, while not low cut, revealed her collarbone. Her neck seemed almost too long.

When she walked out to the kitchen he got up and followed her. She was sitting down at the table and was looking at her hands. Feeling rather self-conscious Lucian set about making a pot of tea. He looked through the cupboards for the materials he needed, but she was oblivious to him.

While waiting for the kettle to boil he stared out of the window, unthinking, and when he poured the water into the pot he asked how she would like her tea. Still she said nothing and he resumed his position at the window. Eventually he decided that it must have brewed so he poured the tea into two cups. His movement now reminded her of his presence.

"I think that Gerald is dead," she said simply.

"How do you know?"

"A quiet feeling of liberation has come over me."

She got up and held out her hand, which he took without questioning her. She took him to the door and to his surprise led him outside. The wind dashed the rain into their faces and roared about in the trees overhead. He hadn't noticed how wild it had become outside. They walked, heads down, around to the front of the house and into the full force of the tempest. It would have been almost impossible to talk, or shout even, but he heard Miranda laugh. He wanted to insist that they go back inside, that it was too cold to be out, but she pulled him forwards and down the lawn to a small exposed terrace where the wind tore at their clothes and tried to push them back uphill. She stopped when they were close to the edge and looked out into the wind. In the uproar he could not see the town below, all points of reference were lost in the riot of wind and rain. It was painful and exhilarating at the same time.

She was still laughing. She seemed out of control.

It was not comfortable to be standing still. He hadn't ever known how drenching and cold the rain could be. He was sodden already. The mud oozed into his shoes, but looking down he could see that Miranda had abandoned hers. She saw him looking at her feet, where the mud came up between her toes. He felt drunk again from the night before, and hung-over, and realised that he didn't quite know what they were doing there. She took his head in her hands and shouted into his ear that she was so cold she could sense her skeleton, and was afraid that if she should fall over then her bones would snap. But all he could think of at that moment was that her words were too loud, but that her breath on his ear felt warm.

And then she let go of him and turned to the rain, and started to sing loudly.

The leaves were torn from the tossing branches of the trees. The wind caused her dress to stream away behind her. It tore through his shirt, separating it from his body by cold, wet blasts.

After a few moments she yelled her explanation; she was trying to out-sing the wind.

She pulled him forward. He wondered how far the gale would take the woman's words. Perhaps not far, for the wind seemed to be constantly changing direction. They might be snatched from her and taken down into the town. They might be borne across the valley as far as the distant hills.

They had to hold on to each other for support as the wind moved round and was now at their backs, forcing them towards the low western wall of the garden and the edge. It pushed them with an insistence that he was unwilling to go along with. At the very top it was all that they could do to turn around and not be thrown over the side.

Miranda suddenly took his head in her hands again, and kissed him on the lips. She gave him no time to respond, but she held him tight and he felt her cold body against his. Again, before he could do anything to reciprocate she turned back to the streaming wind and then she let go of him. The wind seemed to lift him up. He bent to it and was light. He straightened out and on tip-toe, at an angle to the wind, it was as though he had no weight at all. The wind was constant, no longer in gusts, and did not let him down. He put his arms out as if to fly and it seemed to him that there, at the very top of the world with nothing but chaos about them, that he was actually lifted off the ground. He became one with the wind. It moved around him and through him and he was no longer an obstruction to it.

And then the wind let him down, and Lucian collapsed on the muddy ground.

"You were trying to fly," Miranda shouted at him excitedly. "And you do it very well."

He could not stop grinning. She offered a hand to help him up.

"You're filthy," she laughed and hugged him. When she let go he laughed:

"So are you now."

He took a handkerchief out of his pocket and started to wipe the mud from her face.

"No," she said, struggling away. "Let's get back indoors and out of this."

They ran back across the lawn, bent low against the wind, and in at the nearest door, leading into the conservatory. It was not locked and they would have both hurried through the cold studio but they stopped before the portrait on the easel. Lucian was surprised to see that it had been worked on, presumably at some time that day. The figure was the same, but the background had been given detail that made it look like hanging material.

Miranda shivered but could not look away from it. Lucian too was cold, but he was staring at her. He noticed that the ugly mark around her eye had yet deepened in colour. He looked down at her hands and could see blood mixed with the mud.

The din of the rain on the huge glazed roof was immense. He shivered violently and she noticed, grinning and trembling with cold herself.

"Where are his paints?" Lucian asked, rubbing his arms in an attempt to warm them. "Where's the paint brush he'd have been using?"

"I don't know. I can't see them anywhere. He must've taken them away with him," she shivered almost uncontrollably.

"What's he playing at?" Lucian asked. He was staring into the background of the composition. "It must have taken him some time to do this. This painting is quite detailed. It isn't just purple, it's red and mauve . . . There's white mixed in, in faint streaks."

Miranda did not answer. She simply stood hugging her wet clothes to herself and shivered.

"And it's quite dry," he added, poking the canvas with his index finger. He received a slap on the hand from Miranda.

Neither of them said anything.

"It's really quite well done," he continued.

"Don't say anything," she said, stamping her feet in the small puddle of water that had run off her. She could not stop shaking and walked briskly through to the hall.

Lucian followed slowly. He could not help but think that she was collaborating with the artist. Perhaps, he guessed, it was an elaborate game? He could not have eluded them all day and yet have been painting at the same time?

Lucian followed Miranda's damp footsteps upstairs where she was taking a towel from a cupboard.

"Perhaps you ought to keep all the doors locked, then we'd have to hear him coming in," he proposed.

"I never lock the doors," she pointed out, walking to the bathroom but not shutting the door behind her.

"I suppose he'd have had his own key anyway."

From where Lucian stood, talking, he could see her pull her dress off, up over her head. He took a step back.

"There could of course be a supernatural explan-ation," he tried to joke.

"He's somewhere in the house," she called back at him. "He probably never left. He must've been in here all the time."

"But you saw him leave?"

"He hit me and I fell on the ground. Maybe he simply came back? Maybe that's why I couldn't catch up with him?"

"I didn't hear him come back." Lucian had doubts now. He heard the shower turned on and found a towel for himself in the cupboard. He rubbed his hair with it vigorously as he walked into his own room and then started to remove his own sodden clothes. He took out the one spare pair of trousers from his bag and sat on the bed and waited. He would have to take a shower after Miranda and hoped she wouldn't be long; he was shaking with cold.

Eventually the shower was turned off and he heard her go across to her room.

Walking out carefully he didn't look through her open door on his way past.

"I didn't hear him come back," Lucian called back at her. "Why did you run after him? What were you going to do? The bastard hit you."

He turned on the shower and took off his clothes. As he was getting in the shower she appeared, leaning on the doorframe in a long-sleeved, dark red, almost black dress. It was an evening dress for a special occasion; it looked wrong at that moment. She didn't appear to notice his nakedness and embarrassment.

"Oh, my plan was simple . . . I was going to kill him," she said matter-of-factly.

"Fair enough," he said, his back to her as he started to wash. He had long since given up trying to understand her humour. "But that means he's probably in the house with us now?"

"Listening to us, no doubt," she said, then called loudly back into the house: "He's such a bore."

When he looked back she was still in the doorway, looking down at her still wet feet. "I want him to be gone," she said, and finally noticing his embarrassment she walked away.

"You know," he called after her. "You don't have to let him come back. You're not just going to accept his return are you?"

She came back to the door, her expression more serious:

"Our relationship was expedient in many ways. All the best ones are. Love has never come into marriage, at least, not happy marriages. You need to find the right partner for practical, not romantic reasons. Romance is to be found outside marriage, isn't it?"

"I wouldn't know."

"Of course it is! We didn't get married; we both appreciated what a farce it is. People together for a long time begin to hate each other, so you find a partner who doesn't mind being hated, and who enjoys hating the other person. Come on, you can tell me the truth, you hate him as well? Everyone does who has ever met him."

"I don't know him well enough to properly hate him," he said, and then considered that his words might not have sounded quite how he meant them to.

She laughed, but there was a crash from downstairs.

"He's down there," cried Miranda, surprised.

"That explains it," Lucian said, angrily. "Are you a part of the games he's playing?"

"He isn't here!" she contradicted herself, almost screaming at him.

"All right," he said, getting out of the shower and putting a towel around himself. He was too annoyed to think of how he looked at that moment. "You go down the front stairs," he ordered her. "I'll go down the back stairs and we'll meet in the hall. We'll flush him out."

Miranda stood at the head of the stair and yelled, "We're coming to find you." She did not descend, however.

"Come on, let's get this over with." He prompted from the other end of the landing. Still Miranda refused to move.

"You can prove to me that he isn't here," Lucian tried to sound as though he thought it all a great game. "Or that he is. Whatever you want it to be."

"You can look for yourself! I'm not wasting my time chasing after him."

"Come on, Miranda," he tried to look as though he understood what was happening.

"Yeah, sure," and she disappeared unwillingly down into the darkness.

Lucian continued on through the rambling house, throwing on all the lights in the darker corners. Striding from room to room he failed to find the artist. It was the first time he had been in many of the rooms and it was a depressing exercise to see the house in such a state of deterioration. It was not just that the paintwork and wallpaper and long curtains were stained and discoloured with age, but in places plaster had dropped from the walls and ceiling; in some places it still lay where it had fallen. Cobwebs even trailed across the doorways of the least used rooms.

He met Miranda at the front door and advocated that they go back up and repeat the exercise upstairs. He suggested that they must have misheard where the sound had come from. Miranda followed him and he repeated the exercise of turning on all the lights. The loft space was eventually the only place which could possibly have concealed anyone.

"No, he can't be up there," she pointed out. "It'd require athletic skills that the bastard doesn't possess."

"I suppose you're right, and those cobwebs haven't been touched. You should be ashamed of them," he tried to sound light-hearted. Suddenly, now he had stopped running from room to room, he felt cold again.

"If they worry you," she mumbled, distracted, "then there's a brush in the kitchen." She continued to look at the loft hatch.

"I've got slightly better things to do than clear up your cobwebs."

Miranda walked through to her bedroom, calling out to the man hidden somewhere in the house:

"We give up because we couldn't give a shit where you are." She turned to shut the door. "I'll see you downstairs when you're dressed."

"All right. But then I'll leave you two to sort it out between yourselves. I'd better be going home."

"No you're not," she shook her head. "You're not leaving me here alone, with him. It's too late to pack and go home now."

"All right," Lucian conceded meekly. Back in the privacy of the locked bathroom he dried himself, still unnerved that there might be a third person in the house, although he could not imagine where the man could have hidden himself, or why.

Back in his room Lucian put on his spare pair of trousers, but otherwise dressed himself in his previous day's clothes. When he came to return the towel to the bathroom he noticed the pile of muddy clothes that Miranda had left on the floor. He picked them up, thinking to add them to his own and take them all down to the kitchen where he had seen a washing machine. His hands were muddy from handling them, but then he noticed that there was blood on them. He carefully put her things back down again, were he had found them, and returned his own clothes to his room.

⁞

The radio was on quietly and Miranda was starting to prepare some food.

"No Gerald then?" she asked brightly as she chopped up some vegetables.

"No," Lucian agreed. He was standing in the doorway and shouted back over his shoulder: "Well, I'm going to help myself to Gerald's wine. One of the really nice bottles he was boasting about yesterday. And if he's annoyed by that then he can come out and say so himself."

Miranda let out an amused "Ha!" and seemed genuinely more at ease than she had been all weekend.

"Can I help?" Lucian asked, and she pointed to the pile of washing up on the worktop. He went to the sink and filled it with hot water while watching her deftly cut the top off a couple of leeks, then slit them down the side. She stood alongside him as she put them under the running tap and cleaned them out. From under the grill some meat was starting to spit as it cooked, and everything seemed suddenly everyday, quiet and comforting.

"Thanks for staying," she said but would not look at him.

"I'm happy to. At home now my parents would be watching television downstairs and I'd only be up in my room reading. This seems more real. More like living."

"I wouldn't call the last couple of days more real."

"They certainly haven't been boring."

"No, that's true."

"Is he really here?"

"I don't know. But it's like he might be. It's like he's waiting to jump out at us, to give us a fright like we've never had."

"I find it unnerving too."

"But it's more than that. It's been going on for years. Sometimes I run my fingers through my hair and I don't feel my scalp beneath. I feel my skull."

Lucian said he did not understand.

While he washed-up the crockery and glasses she cut up the leeks very small, then heated some butter in a pan and threw them in. When the hissing subsided she turned back to him:

"If I sound morbid it's because of Gerald. I know you don't like him. I hate the bastard, but I did love him once."

"Where did you meet him?"

"At a party. We were all having an argument, or rather, everyone was arguing against him. I didn't join in, I just listened. He was arguing such rubbish with so much passion that I was really quite impressed. At the time I couldn't imagine that he really believed what he was saying. I thought it was an act. It was only later when we started going out together that I understood that he believed those things.

"We dressed in black and pretended to read Aleister Crowley. He made black wax skulls and exhibited them. It was laughable really, though we were both serious enough about it at the time. For him it was a pose from which he moved to another. And then that pose was discarded for another, and then another. But somewhere inside me I'm still as morbid as I was then."

"What did you do while he was making his skulls?"

"Early on I was still at school, but when I left I tried dropping out and writing poetry, but I was still living here with my mother."

"What kind of poetry did you write?"

"It was gloomy in the extreme, which is the most positive thing you can say about it."

"Have you kept any of it?"

"No."

"Of course you have. You're just too much of a coward to read it to me!"

At this she threw a large piece of potato peeling at him.

"I can assure you that it wasn't any good," she insisted.

And so they discussed books, just as they had done on the first night with Gerald, Adrian and Elizabeth. As Lucian and Miranda ate in the dining room later they moved on to music and she played records from her collection to emphasise the greatness or otherwise of music she used to listen to. Her talk was all very much in the past tense however. She had obviously not bought a record for several years. When they returned to the discussion of books she talked of reading as an activity that she had relished in the past.

"What else are we going to do this evening," she asked, getting up and collecting the plates.

"I don't know."

"Not cards" she warned with a grin as she left the room.

Lucian took the chance to phone his parents to say that he was staying a little longer and was very self-conscious when Miranda reappeared from the kitchen with a bottle of wine and two glasses. She waited at the foot of the stairs for him to finish the call, and when he put the receiver down she made no comment but told him to follow her up to her room.

"I know the whole house is mine, but this is my room. It's my cocoon, an environment I can control and feel safe in."

"You're still worried about Gerald?" he asked, stopping on the stair.

"I suppose I am."

"Let me lock the doors and check that everything's secure."

"If it makes you feel better," she agreed and continued on up.

Lucian turned back to the darkened ground floor and was rapidly spooked by the idea that somebody might be there. He threw the bolts at the top and bottom of the front door and checked that the windows were shut tight. He made sure that each room was well-lit before he entered it. He looked around the living room, dining room and kitchen. Only the conservatory was left.

He threw on all the lights half-expecting the artist to jump out at him but it was empty. He was able to lock the doors, and the windows were secure. The lights from inside lit up the first few feet of lawn, but beyond that it was pitch darkness outside. The rain was still loud on the glass but the wind had died down a little. He could sense the movement of the trees, though and tried not to consider that anybody out there would have a clear view of him, but would remain undetected themselves. As he hurried out he glanced at the picture of Miranda and was horrified to see that it had changed once more. Miranda was not there to stop him and this time he felt that the paint was actually wet. The background had been worked on to give the impression of shapes and their shadows, and somebody had worked on the detail of her hair. More colour had also been added to the figure of Miranda. It was an unhealthy colour, as if to imply corruption. Gerald had never painted flesh in a flattering light, but the artist was now working in blue, suggesting that it was under the skin. He made her look not only cold but almost brittle.

The doors may all be locked, but had Lucian perhaps locked Gerald inside? He told himself that he would now have to check where the man might be hiding.

Tentatively he opened a cupboard at the far end of the conservatory but all that was inside was a few coats and shoes and cleaning materials. The next cupboard he pulled open quickly, hoping that if anybody was inside he would have surprise on his side. But once again there was nobody to be found. He checked in the kitchen, the dining room and under the stairs. It was depressing going from decaying room to decaying room, but in each he pulled the dusty curtains tight shut. In the living room there was only one cupboard large enough to conceal a man but it was stacked with books, folders and papers which threatened to fall out.

"What were you up to down there?" Miranda asked when he had finished downstairs and was passing her bedroom door.

"Paranoia. I'm making sure he isn't hiding anywhere."

"If you find him give him a good kicking from me," she called.

He put his head around the door of the guest bedroom where he had not slept the previous night. Tentatively he switched on the light and knelt down so as to be able to see under the bed. Miranda could obviously see him from her room.

"God, you really are paranoid aren't you?"

"Completely."

He checked the other bedrooms and they were similarly tenantless, so he went in to Miranda who was standing in front of the mirror arranging her hair, piling it on top of her head, but allowing some to fall here and there with a certain measured casualness.

"Satisfied?" she asked through the pins she held in her mouth.

"Yes, but I don't understand."

"Some things are best left a mystery."

As she raised her arms again to put the pins through her hair, the long sleeves fell back down her arms far enough to reveal a network of red scars.

"Like why you put up with him so long?" he asked, astounded that he could have done that to her.

"Oh ho! And who are you to pass judgment?"

"I'm sorry."

"Perhaps," she said, turning "we all give the best of our hearts uncritically to those who hardly think about us in return?"

"That sounds like a quote, but I don't know where from."

"T.H. White."

Miranda lay back down on the bed and stretched across for her half-full glass of wine on the bedside table. He took up the full glass next to it and swallowed a large mouthful.

Looking down at her lying there in the grey dress that showed off her figure so well, he wondered if she would allow him to kiss her. The scars on her arms troubled Lucian. All day long he had been close to Miranda but had not dared imagine that she was really interested in him. He sat on the side of the bed, trying to look unconcerned.

"Tell me about yourself," she asked.

"There's not much to tell. I mean, you're the one with the interesting life. You've been places, done things, met people. My life begins when I escape for University and see the world."

"I haven't been anywhere. I've spent my time in this house. But travelling doesn't mean you necessarily see things, or learn anything."

"No, my grandmother once said she had travelled all over the world through the books she borrowed from the library."

"Your grandmother was a wise woman."

"Miranda?"

"Yes?"

"I know this is probably a very silly thing to say, and really bad timing . . . "

She sat up looking slightly amused: "Go on?"

"What with the disasters of Gerald and Elizabeth . . . "

She leant forward and pulled his head towards her softly, smiling, and kissed his cheek. She smelt faintly of perfume, of honey, and her lips were warm. He shivered involuntarily but she did not seem to notice. There was no sound save for the clock chiming, loudly, far down in the house.

She stroked his face and he was moving forward to kiss those beautifully bitten lips when he saw that her hand was smeared with blood. He took it in his own and traced it back up her arm as far as the sleeves would allow him. It was dark and heavy like old port wine.

"Blood," he said dully.

"I cut myself, that's all. Nothing much."

She made to kiss him this time but he pulled away.

Miranda looked serious for a moment then smiled. She lifted her arms and pulled up her sleeves so as to show the long cuts. The smeared blood could not hide the other scars that he had seen earlier.

"Gerald . . . ?" he struggled.

"Me," she said simply. "Self inflicted."

"Oh."

"Do the scars disturb you?" she asked.

Miranda casually pulled her sleeve back down. Without a word she got up and left the room.

&

The quiet sound of clinking cut through a dream that was immediately forgotten. It was the sound of a bottle and glasses. It was dark and for a second Lucian was unable to account for anything. Then he sensed her moving towards him. He had returned unwillingly to his own dark room, unsure of what to do. He had lain down on the bed and must have fallen asleep.

"Drink with me."

"What time is it?"

"Early, late? It's always time for a drink."

"There's something we ought to talk about."

"I assumed you'd want to."

He sat up and Miranda handed him a glass. She poured the drink and in the darkness spilt some of it over his hands. He heard her gulp down the liquid that he pretended to sip. It was whisky.

"Why do you cut yourself?"

Miranda did not answer. She put the bottle down and walked back over to the door. Lucian thought he'd offended her again but she turned on the landing light so as to borrow some illumination. When she came back in she sat down beside him on the bed.

"Do you enjoy the pain?" he asked carefully.

"No, not in itself," she shook her head.

He waited for her to continue, which she did only after some time.

"It's not the pain. It's the power over the pain. When I have a knife and press it to my skin I can choose whether or not to hurt myself. It's like smoking or drinking. I'm in control."

"But you aren't. Look at your arms."

"I am in control," she repeated. "Usually I don't cut myself. But when I do I can control the degree of pain. The pain is less frightening because I can stop it at any time. Fear is half of pain, the worst half; it hurts most when you have no idea of when it'll stop, if it'll ever stop."

He shook his head: "But it's destructive. How can you be in a position of power when you're hurting yourself?"

"It's power over myself. It's hard to explain."

A pause.

"Imagine two people," she decided upon her illustration, "with power over each other, equal power. Say one is myself, the other my 'perfect partner'. If we are in perfect sympathy, if I can trust him totally, there would be no fear if he had a knife against my skin. He would know whether I wanted to be cut. And if I wanted him to apply pressure he would know. If the pain was too much he would stop, without me saying a word. Perfect trust, perfect knowledge."

"And you and Gerald were like that?"

"No," she shook her head. "I would never have trusted him. I've only ever trusted myself. I have to have that trust of myself."

"But you can't control it. You aren't in control. It *is* like smoking."

"It's not that you don't understand," she frowned. "It's that you can't understand. I've explained it well enough. And the smoking isn't an addiction. I smoke herbal cigarettes. There's no nicotine. No, the cutting is almost like a meditative thing. It's a discipline."

"It can't be a discipline, though . . . "

"But it is. It's like fasting, stopping yourself from eating. You crave food but you use will power to deny yourself. You do go back to food, you have to. But there would be no discipline if there wasn't the real possibility that I'd cut myself sometimes."

"But is the cutting analogous to the eating or the fasting? Is the cutting or the 'not cutting' the necessity of life?"

She shrugged:

"I don't know. One can't exist without the other. You can't say that you exercised will power to make yourself not cut, not if you never had the intention of cutting in the first place."

There was another uncomfortable silence. He needed to know. He wanted to help:

"Why do you fell the need to exercise this 'discipline'? Why do you need to have this control?"

She considered.

"Perhaps that's the relevant question. But you're frightened by the idea of me hurting myself. Would you be less frightened if we stopped talking about it? Would you be less frightened if I were someone you didn't know? Would you be less frightened if the pain was far removed from your experience?"

"You're trying to say that I fear it if it's close to me?"

"That you're frightened of the pain happening to you? That you might do the same to yourself?"

"You're wrong."

"Really? It's as simple as that is it?"

"Yes."

"Come with me," she insisted, rising and dragging him up off the bed after her. She kept hold of his hand and took him downstairs to the cold kitchen. She threw on the light and only then did it dawn on him what might happen next.

Miranda took a knife from the drawer and offered it to him. He took it automatically and she pulled up the sleeve of her dress and offered her arm to him. Miranda took his hand and held the knife to her own skin.

"Who are you afraid of hurting, me or yourself?"

"You, of course!" he said, angry.

He pulled away but Miranda still held his hand and the knife made a thin line appear on her skin. Little points of blood appeared down its length. He was horrified by what she had made him do. They stood looking at her arm.

"I'm so sorry," she said, "I shouldn't have done that to you."

It seemed an odd thing to say; he was confused and couldn't think of a suitable reply. They stayed in that awkward position until she moved away from him and ran her arm under the cold tap. It made her draw in her breath sharply, and the tainted water ran into the sink

"Our drinks are upstairs," she noted.

"I don't much like whisky," he admitted.

"Let me get you something else," and she was suddenly the good hostess. Drying her arm on a towel she added: "I would offer you port, but I don't think there's any left. You said you wanted some of Gerald's wine?"

"I was just saying it to annoy him. Don't open a bottle just for me."

"Vodka? Absinthe?"

"I've never had absinthe, but no, not tonight, it's too late."

"Don't be stupid. Not had absinthe? You shall be educated."

He was surprised that rather than directing him to a bottle of spirits she asked him to pass a small glass jug which she filled with water. Then she took his hand with a mischievous smile and pulled him into the living room. From the darkness of the old sideboard she produced a bottle of highly-synthetic looking green liquid which she passed to him while she found two glasses.

And then she enacted an age-old decadent ritual. A generous measure of the absinthe was poured into each slightly dirty glass, and then with an elegant curve of her arm she let the water drop from the jug in an almost infinitely slow but steady trickle. The green liquid turned cloudy, opalescent in one glass, and then in the other.

"You can pour it over sugar," she explained. "Gerald did have a specially perforated spoon but it was lost."

She held the glass up for Lucian and he marvelled at the eddies of swirling liquid as the reaction finished. In the light of the red-draped room the drink was the colour of jade. He sipped it hopefully but decided that it was horrible, like aniseed or liquorice. He dutifully took another small sip and decided that perhaps it was not entirely unpalatable.

"There're lots of rituals associated with absinthe," she continued her lecture.

"Can't you set light to it?"

"Only if you're a complete idiot and want to lose the alcohol."

"Which rituals do you prefer?"

"I only drink it when I'm already drunk. And I pour it in a proportion of four to one. And it's best drunk in bed."

"Why in bed?"

"Because it affects my ability to stand up. If I collapse I'll be more comfortable if I happen to be lying in bed already."

He dutifully followed her upstairs.

"Gerald introduced me to it," she said as they moved quietly through the house, glasses in hand. "He had to drink it because Baudelaire did. But I came to love it because Ernest Dowson drank it."

And she lay on the bed in the dark room and started to lecture him on the decadents of the 1890s.

"But there're slightly more important things to talk about," Lucian said, embarrassed by his pomposity. He sat on the bed with her.

"Like what? Me cutting myself?"

"I'd be concerned at anyone doing it."

"Really?"

"No, not entirely," he considered. "I've only known you a few days, but I do care about you."

"Do you love me?"

He hesitated long enough for Miranda to think:

"You care for me," she conceded. "But how much? What's between us?'

"Gerald?" he asked, not sure if he was being clever.

"Why?"

"I don't know. I don't like him, and I can't see what you liked in him. Sorry," he corrected himself, "why you *loved* him."

"And that's important to you?"

"I suppose so."

"Well, that's okay. I never really loved him. He was a bore. He *is* a bore; especially at the moment."

Lucian looked into Miranda's face. It was lit by the far away light of the bulb on the landing:

"What do you feel for me?" he asked.

"Not love," she admitted immediately.

He was not sure whether he was relieved or hurt.

"Would you like to make love to me?" she asked.

"Yes, but not now."

"That's fine," she said. "Get into bed. We'll finish our drinks and try to get some sleep."

He walked around to the far side of the room and sat down on the bed with his back to her. As he undid the belt of his trousers he felt the bed move as she got up off it. She walked to the wardrobe and he could see her, out of the corner of his eye, slip off her dress and hang it up. He couldn't help but be excited by her white, lovely body in her black underwear. He didn't know whether he should be watching, or how many of his clothes he should remove. She had asked if he wanted to make love, which seemed to give him more freedom, but he didn't turn around as she walked to the door and switched off the light in the hall. He took off the rest of his clothes and slipped inside the crumpled mess of sheets after her.

She lay still next to him and they both finished their absinthes in silence. Then she took his glass and put it with hers on the bedside table. He did not move, and hardly breathed. She changed position once and then a minute later he heard her breathing slow down and become deeper. There was a sound in the walls and he wondered if there were rats, or at least mice. She had fallen asleep in minutes, but it took him longer to drift into unconsciousness. She was warm next to him and he was excited, but dared not move.

৪৩

There was a scream the next morning. It woke Lucian, but he had been so heavily asleep that he was not sure whether to trust his senses. He had become conscious so quickly that he could remember what he had been dreaming about with startling clarity: Miranda was lying in water; she was covered with leaves and weed, her clothes hanging about her unmoving form, heavy, taking her shape and making her look fragile and skinny. The colouring of his dream was corrupt, like her skin in the portrait. He could see not only the black blood of her cuts, but the slight colour of bruise just under the white surface of her skin. And her eyes, he had dreamed, were open and slightly bloodshot, not with red but with violet.

He remembered the picture and the scream made sense. As he guessed it would, his head hurt once again from the alcohol of the night before. He took the dressing gown from the hook on the back of her door. According to a little bedside clock it was twenty to ten already.

It was still dark in the house for none of the heavy curtains had been opened from the night before. Through the ironwork of the banister there was a dim glow from downstairs. More vague sounds came up to him and he was loath to investigate.

He quietly descended the stairs, identifying the noise as a sobbing that would not have been out of place in an amateur melodrama. It was a sound that made him think again before investigating. Then there was a distant but distinctive "Shit!" that had to have been from Miranda. As he got to the bottom, the swearing came again.

From the hall he could see her in the conservatory. He could see a white face and dark-rimmed eyes as she stood before the painting, staring fixedly at it. She did not react at all to his appearance. He walked in and around the canvas and was surprised to see that it had been worked on once more. The red hair was even brighter, more unreal.

Miranda stood engrossed. He leant against a bleached wicker chair that creaked and she jumped almost a foot into the air. She stared at him without recognition, petrified, and then she collected herself:

"You gave me a fright."

"Sorry," he grinned and then nodded in the direction of the canvas; "The great artist really has returned then?"

"I haven't heard him. And I haven't slept."

"I did, but not well."

"Great!" she was annoyed, her eyes returning to the canvas. "So he can creep in and out of here and us not know about it."

"It appears so."

Lucian peered at the portrait and was disconcerted to find that there was a touch of blue to the model's lips. And there was more of decay and corruption than he had realised. The line, the way that the figure had been drawn, was not quite perfect, but the strangeness seemed to have a purpose. When he looked closely the colour of the skin also had the bruised pallor of purple and yellow which made it even more disconcerting.

He then looked at Miranda herself. The small scab on the side of her head was healing but her eye was now noticeably very bruised. She noticed him staring and he turned away and walked to the windows. He looked out into the Monday morning; great drapes of mist hung about the Downs and lay over the town below. The trees appeared dark and dripping out of the mist like huge bathers that had been out swimming all night. He peered through them to where the town should be and it felt very strange that he was not a part of it.

They ate breakfast with few words between them. Lucian was feeling a little better having taken a couple of pills for his hangover. He remarked that he liked Miranda's dress, a tatty black creation of old silk.

"Gerald bought it for me. It's meant to've belonged to Queen Victoria."

"Really?"

"Probably not, no," she replied without humour.

An awkward silence followed breakfast, and she left the room so that afterwards he washed up alone. He waited a while before going up to her room to find his clothes. Miranda was in the bathroom so he dressed and waited for her to finish. He laid on her bed but she seemed to be taking a very long time and he could hear nothing.

He decided to give her twenty minutes by the bedside clock and when that painfully long period was over he went to the door and knocked quietly. She did not answer.

"Miranda, are you all right?" he asked.

There was still no answer, and now he listened. A sharp intake of breath was audible from inside, and instantly he knew what she was doing.

He stood back from the door and considered breaking it down. Could he do it, he thought, if he put all of his weight against it? Would he go flying inside if the lock was weak? Then he remembered that he had not even tried the handle.

He opened the door and saw Miranda leaning over the bath. She had her dress pulled down to her waist and she was cutting herself. Lucian was unable to move. There was so much blood that he couldn't see at first what she was using to cut herself.

He moved around behind her, leant over and grasped her hands, pulling the left hand holding the blade away from her bleeding right arm. She cried and dropped what he saw to be a part of his own razor. She moved around on her knees, pulling herself from his grasp easily as his hands were greasy with her blood. She looked angry and in terror he hugged her to himself, not looking at her face but keeping her arms apart.

She was so heavy to drag upright, and when he looked around for something to stop her bleeding could see only a towel. He reasoned that it would be too absorbent to staunch the flow of blood. He tried to pull her after him back into the hall, but her reaction was to stay where she was. He pulled harder, violently this time, angry, and she almost fell after him. She was crying but he managed to half-drag her into the bedroom and pulled the sheet from the unmade bed. He had an idea that he would tear it into strips for bandages but he couldn't rip it with his hands. Miranda sat on the bed and stared at him, and whimpered, the blood continuing to pour down the arms that she held out before her.

Lucian grabbed a pair of scissors from a chair and a few quick cuts enabled him to then rip the sheet into a number of long lengths of bandage. Her arms were still out towards him and he wildly and inefficiently bound them tightly with the sheet. The material darkened almost immediately so he added more and she moaned that he was hurting her.

"I'm calling an ambulance," he told her, ineffectually pulling her dress back up over her breasts.

"No," she pleaded and tried to grab him but her arms would not bend properly.

"I'm sorry for being so stupid. I'm sorry, sorry," she shouted after him as he backed out onto the landing. "Don't phone. They're not deep cuts. I can't cut that deep. I never cut that deep."

"You might've cut an artery," he stood his ground, ready to bound down the stairs to where he could see the phone. She stood up from the bed, pathetically bedraggled, her arms out before her, bound in the bloodied rags.

"I don't need an ambulance. I just need someone to tell me I didn't kill Gerald and that everything is all right, and that I'm not evil."

He hoped she was right about the cuts, but he was not sure that she didn't need the help of someone who knew what they were doing. He was relying on the fact that he had seen the old cuts and scars and she had obviously done this before. He had never imagined there could be so much blood . . .

Lucian walked back in to her and she allowed him to hold her close, and when he pulled away to look into her face she looked at him imploringly, with swollen eyes. Her lips pouted pathetically and he kissed them, more passionately than he had meant to, but she did not respond. It seemed darker in her room than it had done before.

"Your shirt is covered in blood," she pointed out, laughing nervously through her tears.

"It doesn't matter," he said generously.

"You've got to untie some of these bandages," she snivelled, shaking her head. "My arms ache. I think you've cut off the circulation."

He was horrified to see that her hands were turning black, and started to fumble with the knots he had made. Some of them had to be snipped off with the scissors and he laughed nervously. She also started to laugh and he was worried she might become hysterical.

"You're a complete mess," he told her.

"Thanks for the sympathy."

"These cuts'll start bleeding again if I take off all the bandages."

"I told you, they're not deep. Just don't tie them so tight."

They both calmed down in the several minutes it took to bandage her arms properly. When he had finished she lay down on the bed and he lay next to her.

"Oh Miranda, when will you understand how much I love you?"

"I know, I know," she said, burying her face into his neck. "And I've taken advantage of your kindness, your love. But what I need from you is your support."

"Anything."

"Then just lie here with me and tell me that everything will be all right."

"Everything will be all right," he assured her. "I love you, Miranda. And I want to help you."

"I know. But I don't love you," she admitted quietly. "And you don't really love me."

"You can't say that."

"I can. You feel pity and lust."

"That's unfair."

"It's honest."

"And you know all about honesty?"

"I do feel something for you," she admitted quietly. "Perhaps something special did happen here between us."

"I'm not going to deceive myself."

"You don't have to. We didn't need to have sex," she said, but he was not sure whether she was being patronising. "Sex is nothing in itself; it can only confirm something else, other feelings, good or bad."

He turned away from her but she lay against him. In the quiet he became aware of the rain once more on the window pane. Quietly she recited:

"Nous aurons des lits pleins d'odeurs légères,
Des divans profonds comme des tombeaux,
Et d'étranges fleurs sur des étagères,
Ecloses pour nous sous des cieux plus beaux."

"What was that?" he asked her.

"Baudelaire." She translated for him:

"We shall have beds full of gay perfumes,
Divans as deep as graves,
And wondrous flowers displayed on shelves,
Blooming for us beneath more lovely skies."

He wanted to turn to her, to kiss her, but could not move.
Again she recited:

"L'un t'éclaire avec son ardeur,
L'autre en toi met son deuil, Nature!
Ce qui dit à l'un: Sépulture!
Dit à l'autre: Vie et splendeur!"

"One man lights you with his love?" he attempted.

"One man illuminates you with his ardour,
Another sets in you his sorrow, O Nature.
What spells the Grave to one,
Spells life and splendour to the other."

"Everything will be all right, won't it?" she asked.

"Yes," he said with as much gravity as he could muster.
"But you must stop cutting yourself," he added, sounding
stupid to himself, and happy that she could not see his
face. She did not immediately reply and he wondered if
she was asleep. Eventually she said:

"It's not that easy."

"It must be possible to get help?"

"Only if I want it."

"But you can't want to cut yourself?"

"There're worse things I could do."

"But the pain?"

"It's not the pain, I told you before."

"But in the long run," he floundered.

"You can't always think of the next day. You can't always think of tomorrow, because it might never come. People save and invest and die before they can realise anything that they thought they were working towards."

"But that's not the point. No matter how you explain or justify it, it still hurts."

"Not always."

From where he lay he had his back to the window. It became even darker and the rain came harder.

"What did Gerald think of you cutting yourself?"

He felt her body go taut.

"I don't want to talk about Gerald," she said.

"But I still don't understand."

"Good, don't try. I don't want you hurt."

"Oh Miranda."

"What is it that you want from me?" she asked.

"I don't know. In the past I've always wanted some sort of commitment," he admitted.

"And what if I tell you that I don't?"

"That I mean nothing to you?" he finished for her.

"No, you mean nothing to me, not really."

A few seconds later she added dejectedly:

"That isn't true. Not really."

"I'm going away very soon anyway."

"You should."

They lay still for a long time. Again he was not sure whether Miranda was awake all the time. He was not particularly tired but did finally succumb to a fitful and uncertain sleep. He was unable to remember much detail when he did wake but he knew he had dreamed of darkness and vague, huge shapes flailing slowly at an unimaginable distance. These dreams were broken when he occasionally returned to consciousness, but then he would fall asleep again and go back to them. When he finally awoke it was slowly, so slowly that he continued to imagine that he was down on a distant sea-bed. He had been down so far below that the sun never reached him, and the only light was the phosphorescence of the debris that had fallen so slowly down from such a great height, and over such a great time. The pressure of all the water was immense.

And on waking he found himself thrashing around; drowning. Unable to breathe, he was wound up in the bedclothes, and Miranda was lying in his arms, half on him. He woke her up as he moved and she whined and cried at her wounds. It took a few moments before he appreciated that she had continued to bleed and that the blood had dried between the two of them and the sheets. He calmed her by holding her tight and promising to move as carefully as he could. Somehow they got up together and extricated themselves from the sheets. Her arm had been down his side and was fused to him with dried blood. He pulled his own shirt off and helped her out and into the bathroom. She sat on the side of the bath as he ran water in the sink and used a flannel to sponge the material that had stuck to her arms. Slowly it came away, and only a few of the cuts bled badly. She told him where to find some proper dressings in the airing cupboard and she allowed him to bathe her cuts and bind them up. Not one word then passed between them until this was done. Then he knelt down in front of her and took her hands.

"I'm sorry," she said. "You were meant to come for a weekend, to the house you'd fantasised about. What was it you said? 'All decay and grandeur'?"

"Yes, high ceilings, high ideals . . . "

"The air rich with obscenities and the talk of art?"

"Is that a quote?"

"No. I was trying to help conjure up an atmosphere of decadence. And you were meant to be spending time with Elizabeth."

"Perhaps it was never going to work out, long term," he shrugged.

"Perhaps not, but I've spoiled a weekend of lovemaking."

"Maybe it was never going to be any more than that."

"And what's wrong with that? What's wrong with enjoying sex for its own sake? If it's tender, and loving? Oh, ignore me. I can't keep making pronouncements for you."

"But you seem to make sense."

"Do I? Surely if I knew any of the answers I wouldn't be in such a mess? Don't listen to anything I say. Or, yes, listen, and then do the opposite."

"I can help you."

"How, when I can't help myself? No, you'd best leave. I give you my word, my most solemn promise, that I'll see a doctor, and I won't cut myself again."

"Ever?"

"If that's what you want. I promise."

Lucian washed the blood off his hands and Miranda wandered out of the bathroom. He heard her walking down the stairs but did not think about what she might be doing, or where she was going. When he went to find a shirt he had to take an old, crumpled one out of his bag. It was damp from the other clothes he had stuffed in there, and none of them smelt too good. He was wondering how he would explain the state of some of them to his mother; he really would have to go home and get a change of clothes. As he was rummaging through them, wondering which could be aired and worn again he heard Miranda say something from somewhere below, but he could not work out from which part of the house the sound had come; it had been quiet and perhaps not meant for his ears. Nevertheless there had been something wrong about the sound, and with reluctance he left his room and went to find her, buttoning up his shirt as he went.

It was cold down in the hall. He could hear the wind at the back of the house and guessed that the French doors had to have been opened in the studio. He hurried through wondering why she might have gone outside, and in the studio his guess was shown to be correct. He walked over to look outside and perhaps close them, but he noticed that the painting on the easel had been moved. He had to walk around it before he could see that the picture had now taken on the most appalling aspect. The colours of corruption had been heightened in blues and purples. There were also three dark red slashes of paint, like knife wounds, but these were across the entire picture, across the figure and the background, and were obviously just wanton vandalism.

He stepped back and his attention was drawn, by the door banging in the wind, to the cold garden outside. He went over and looked out but could not see Miranda. He knew that the end to everything that had been happening was coming closer, but he did not feel at all panicked or frightened. His veins pumped with adrenalin, but with a strange calmness he went back inside and pulled on his wet shoes and found a coat for himself. Miranda's was still hanging up so he took hers as well.

Outside he realised that he had no idea of where she had gone. He walked to the little terrace overlooking the town but there was no sign of her there. Looking down she had not thrown herself off the side, and he was looking around the garden when a movement in the distance caught his attention. Through the trees, down the road that served as the drive, he had seen something moving and knew it was her.

He ran now, but his strides were measured so that he did not get out of breath. He didn't want to slip on the wet leaves and loose stones, and chose where to place his feet with care among the potholes. At the bottom Lucian could see that she had crossed the road and was walking past the garage back towards the town. She was only wearing her dress and even from a distance she looked bedraggled and strange with the dirty bandages hanging loosely about her arms. One had unwound slightly and trailed after her.

Lucian crossed the road and jogged after Miranda, getting closer although her stride was fast and purposeful. He couldn't quite believe that the cars and lorries could keep passing along the road without anyone stopping to help her; it had to be obvious that she was in distress. He was only a few yards behind her when she disappeared into an alley between two shops.

The busy road was suddenly far away. Their path led to a small court, noisome with the stench of the overflowing bins from the rear of the shops. He entered in time to see her awkwardly step over a broken wooden fence and start walking along the side of the river. When he was over it himself she was then but three feet from him, standing by the river.

She had her back to him as she looked down a muddy bank to the wide river. Lucian walked up to her carefully and she did not seem at all surprised to find that he was there. He took her cold hand in his and pressed it, but received no response. And then he looked down to where she stared. There was a strange shape in the mud, and he distinguished the shape of a head. The hair was matted with mud and it wasn't quite the shape it should have been

Lucian could only just restrain himself from retching. His balance went slightly awry, his legs felt weak and he held on to Miranda to steady himself. She looked at him, slightly reluctantly, and only then seemed to properly recognise him. She smiled weakly, as though comforted by his presence.

"Who's that?" he asked nervously, pointing to the body.

"Can't you guess?"

Miranda's skin was white with an unhealthy glow. Her eyes were dark-shadowed, and though she should have been frozen she did not shiver or appear to feel the cold.

"Is it him? When . . . ?"

"I followed him after he left the house, and I called him all sorts of stupid names. We ended up out there in the road and it was dark and cold and windy and raining. I remember that he looked around him, very carefully to make sure there was nobody about. The night had turned so horrible that there was never going to be anyone out there to see what happened.

"So he punched me in the face," she continued, and then paused, composing herself. "I fell over, but I was already so angry that I didn't notice the pain. I carried on swearing at him, taunting him for hitting me, so he then hit me really hard. He punched me in the stomach with all of his strength and I thought I was going to die. I can still remember the feeling. I was sick. I remember it raining so hard, and being so fucking cold. I was crouching in the middle of the road and he was looking down at me, laughing."

She paused again. "And then he dragged me down here, to the river. I don't know what he intended to do. I fell over. There was a brick on the ground and I picked it up. I was going to smash his skull in, but I knew that I'd have had to raise both of my hands over my head to do it. He'd have seen it coming. But at least it would've been more like manslaughter if I'd succeeded. I would've simply been reacting to his attack on me. But I was more calculating.

And I was feeling so awful and so weak. So I got up with it behind my back. I waited until I could breathe properly again, and then with both hands I pushed it in his face with all my weight behind it.

"He put his hands up but not quick enough. He fell back and, I don't know, twisted somehow."

She frowned and shook her head. "He must've landed awkwardly, hitting his face on that wall down there. He rolled over it and went down into the river with a splash, and that was it. I threw the brick in after him and ran back up to the house."

"So it was an accident?" Lucian asked.

"No, I meant to kill the bastard," she looked up at him. "I suppose I only really succeeded because he hit his head and went over the wall, but it was my fault, and I wanted him dead."

"But if you hadn't killed him, he'd probably have killed you?" he asked.

"No, he'd have known when to stop. He would have dragged me back up to the house and dumped me on the doorstep, but I'd have been alive."

Miranda now opened and closed her mouth, not to speak, but to cry, though she was forcing herself not to. She was looking around wildly as if remembering the incidents of that night and trying to relate them to what she could now see around her in daylight. "It was . . . low tide . . . then," she continued, distraught and distracted. He was unable to think of anything he could say.

She took a deep breath and forced an unrealistic smile.

"I'll have to start painting under your name now."

"Why?" he asked lamely.

"Because in your card game you won his talent from him . . . Only, he didn't have any, of course."

"So I've not won anything of value?"

"From him, no."

"From you? Are you saying that you've done all the painting for him?"

"Of course. I've done it all. That is, until he died."

She looked back down at the body.

"I thought the tide would take him away . . . or drag the mud over him. I thought that it would bury him deeper. But the tide just seems to keep moving him around . . . "

Acknowledgements

With many thanks to Rosalie Parker,
Jim Rockhill, Lidwine de Royer, Dan T. Ghetu,
Mark Valentine, and Brian J. Showers.

ℰꙩ

Putting the Pieces in Place
was originally published in January 2009
by Ex Occidente Press, Bucharest, Romania.

Bloody Baudelaire was originally
published in June 2009
by Ex Occidente Press, Bucharest, Romania.

About the Author

R. B. Russell is the author of a number of novels, novellas, and short story collections, as well as non-fiction on bookish subjects. He is a publisher, and lives in North Yorkshire with his partner, Rosalie Parker.

SWAN RIVER PRESS

Founded in 2003, Swan River Press is an independent publishing company, based in Dublin, Ireland, dedicated to gothic, supernatural, and fantastic literature. We specialise in limited edition hardbacks, publishing fiction from around the world with an emphasis on Ireland's contributions to the genre.

www.swanriverpress.ie

*"Handsome, beautifully made volumes . . .
altogether irresistible."*

– Michael Dirda, *Washington Post*

*"It [is] often down to small, independent, specialist presses
to keep the candle of horror fiction flickering . . . "*

– Darryl Jones, *Irish Times*

*"Swan River Press has emerged as one of the most inspiring
new presses over the past decade. Not only are the books
beautifully presented and professionally produced, but they
aspire consistently to high literary quality and originality,
ranging from current writers of supernatural/weird fiction
to rare or forgotten works by departed authors."*

– Peter Bell, *Ghosts & Scholars*

THE DARK RETURN OF TIME

R. B. Russell

*"I was searching for The Dark Return of Time on the 'net.
It's odd, but there isn't a copy for sale anywhere, and
it doesn't turn up on the British Library catalogue, the
Library of Congress website, or the Biblioteque Nationale."*

The past doesn't always stay where it should. It is as though somebody, or something, is forever trying to bring it painfully into the present.

Flavian Bennett is trying to leave his past behind when he goes to work in his father's bookshop in Paris. But a curious customer, Reginald Hopper, is desperate to resurrect his own murky origins. Hopper believes that a rare and mysterious book, The Dark Return of Time, may be the key to what happened before he arrived in Paris. In this quiet thriller by R. B. Russell, the futures—and pasts—of these two men will soon cross.

"A beautifully written and very clever work of art."

– Black Static

"R. B. Russell's The Dark Return of Time . . .
*is a short thriller that opens in a shop selling
second-hand books in Paris. What could be better?"*

– Michael Dirda, *Washington Post*

SPARKS FROM THE FIRE

Rosalie Parker

The stories in *Sparks from the Fire* explore a wide variety of familiar characters and settings, yet there is always something else—a shadow world that haunts, disturbs, and threatens. Sons and daughters, mothers and fathers, recluses and lovers—all find themselves shifting between realities: the prosaic and the mystical, even between life and death. The horrors and wonders of these parallel existences are often glimpsed, sometimes revealed, and occasionally overwhelm. These nineteen tales inhabit a terrain in which the uncanny may at any time intrude into everyday life.

"[Parker's] treatment of the fantastic is often so light and ambiguous that stories in which it does manifest are of a piece with tales such as 'Jetsam' and 'Job Start', sensitive character sketches whose celebration of life's unforeseen surprises will appeal to fantasy fans as much as the book's more overtly uncanny tales. Parker proves herself a subtle and versatile writer."

– Publishers Weekly

"If you prefer spending dark evenings with a single author, consider . . . Rosalie Parker's Sparks From the Fire, *which collects nineteen stories, some set against the brooding Yorkshire landscape."*

– Michael Dirda, *Washington Post*

DEATH MAKES
STRANGERS OF US ALL

R. B. Russell

At the edges of everyday life, on geographical boundaries and in the margins of society, certainties and realities can wear thin. And if we find ourselves in such occult and outland territory late at night, we might glimpse phenomena out of the corner of our eye that cannot possibly be there. At such times even the past, apparently fixed and unchanging in memories and dreams, cannot be relied upon.

But what happens if we find ourselves passing beyond even these frayed perimeters of life? Can others follow us, or are we on our own? And just where will our final journey take us? How can we perceive or understand the changes that death will bring?

*"The disorienting title story of R. B. Russell's superb
Death Makes Strangers of Us All takes us into
an 'unreal city' straight out of Kafka or Borges."*

– Michael Dirda, *Washington Post*

*"Once again, R. B. Russell has produced
a fine collection of remarkable stories
told in a captivating, styling fashion."*

– Mario Guslandi